The Case of The Magic Fluke

A **Millicent Winthrop** Novel: Book 6

by

Gwen Overland

writing as

Cunigunda Valentine

NINE WAVES MEDIA

Acknowledgements

To my trusted writer friend, Cynthia Rogan, thank you for taking the time to read my work and for providing valuable feedback.

And to Marisa Brown at Venus Promotions for her constant attention to the marketing of myself and my books.

A huge thanks to Rhian Awni for my extraordinary, playful cover art.

And as always, a huge thanks to my devoted family, who never seem to mind the hours I spend away from them doing what I love second to them.

And a special thanks to my late maternal grandmother, whose name I've lovingly appropriated as my pseudonym.

Dedication

To my adorable grandson, Erik Overland, born December 4th, 2019, without whose inspiration I would not have thought to give Millicent and Alfredo the gift of a baby.

Prologue

Watson slowly raised his sleepy little black pug head from off his comfortable pillow, which had now become his bed since earlier that year he, his littermate Holmes, and his mistress Millicent had moved in with her new husband, Alfredo, whose long-time family home was located in the Dorsoduro sestieri of Venice, Italy. Holmes was likewise lying on his matching pillow bed, yet unlike Watson, was completely out cold and snoring as loudly as a buzzsaw in a lumber yard. Whatever that was, thought Watson, having never in his short life seen a buzzsaw nor a lumber yard, for that matter. But Millicent had once accused Alfredo of sounding much the same in his sleep, so in Watson's thinking there had to be some truth to it.

"'olmes, psst," Watson whispered in his signature Cockney accent, "you awake?"

Immediately, Holmes sprang up out of his make-shift bed, his eyes wide open against his black muzzle and fawn-colored fur. "What? Who's there?" he asked, startled half out of his wits.

"It's only me, 'olmes," Watson continued.

"I know 'it's only you'," Holmes answered in a huff, facing over to where he guessed his all-too-annoying brother lay. "For heaven's sake, Watson. It's still dark out—go back to sleep."

"But I can't," he whined.

Now that Alfredo no longer treated psychiatric patients, the boys' beds took up most of the small room that had once been his office—an ideal distance from Millicent and Alfredo's bedroom, also located down the second floor hall but to the right.

Holmes circled his bed three times before plopping down into his favorite position—front legs stretched out in front of him, his pug mug resting on top. "Yes, I know. Yet I can, so lay your head back down on your pillow, close your eyes, and think happy, restful thoughts."

"But—"

"No buts about it, Watson. Morning will come soon enough, and then we can play to our hearts' content."

"But I wanna play now," Watson pressed.

"Good night, Watson," Holmes said, all but ignoring him. "You'll need all your energy tomorrow to keep up with your usual brand of high-jinx."

"Oh, all right," he acquiesced and turned over several times until he found a comfortable place to stretch out. Following Holmes's orders, he then closed his eyes and thought about those things which gave him the most pleasure—sitting in Millicent's lap, chasing butterflies, and, of course, food. And not just any food, but heavenly things like, batter fried sardines, ricotta stuffed cannoli, and, his favorite—spicy pepperoni pizza, or as they call it in Venezia, pizza al salame piccante.

He'd barely had time to enjoy his blissful imaginings when he heard his stomach growl. Instantly, his eyes flew open, and without thinking he once again howled, "'olmes, I'm 'ungry."

"Bugger all, Watson," Holmes snapped. "Why can't you put a bloody sock in it and belt up?"

"Sorry 'olmes. I can't 'elp it," he said and started to cry. "I don't know what my problem is tonight, but I'm feeling quite restless."

"Oh, bother," Holmes said with a yawn. Watson could tell by the sound of Holmes's voice that he was beginning to relent, so he in turn released one more pitiful sob.

"Look, don't cry, Watson," Holmes pleaded. "Just trot over here and snuggle in with me. The truth is, I've been feeling somewhat antsy myself lately. Maybe together we can calm each other down and finish out our

3

night's sleep. How does that sound to you?"

"Right brilliant, 'olmes," he said, racing across the floor before cozying up to his brother. "I knew I could count on you, 'olmes."

"Yes, yes," Holmes sighed and scooted toward one edge of the pillow so as to make room for Watson, who although smaller always seemed to take up most of the bed. "And please turn yourself around, Watson. I for one do not want to see your back end in my face first thing in the morning."

"Oh, yes, of course. Gotcha, 'olmes," Watson whispered as he repositioned himself. "Good night, 'olmes and thank you."

"You're welcome. Now, no more talking," Holmes firmly announced.

"I won't, 'olmes. Not another word."

"Good," Holmes answered, clearly nodding off.

"If I feel like I need to say something," Watson continued, "I'll make sure I do so very softly. You won't hear another word from me. I promise."

The only thing Watson heard Holmes mumble in return was the word gelato—a response he often uttered when drifting off to sleep. And sometimes also in the middle of the night. Two, maybe three times, in fact.

In many ways, hearing Holmes talk in his sleep as he often did, mentioning delicious and enticing food items, made Watson feel a sense of security and comradeship with his fellow littermate. Unfortunately, however, it also conjured up images of said items in his already overly-stimulated imagination, and before he knew it, Watson was salivating as his stomach once again growled in agonizing rumbles.

Now, it wasn't altogether his fault. After all, Holmes had told him to think of pleasant and happy thoughts. And for Watson that more often than not involved sweets. And his favorite dessert item of all was lemon flavored gelato.

"Al limon," he sighed, eyes closed and with a slight grin forming on his distinctive, white-whiskered push face.

"Gelato," Holmes mumbled again on an exhale, and again Watson followed with "al limon."

Before either pug realized it, their breathing had become synchronized, and all that could be heard emanating from that small make-shift bed was the hypnotic chant of gelato al limon. That was until Watson woke with a start.

"'olmes," he blurted, "I know now why I can't sleep."

"Bloody hell, Watson," Holmes whined, "I was right in the middle of my favorite dream, licking a double scoop cone of lemon gelato."

"Sorry 'olmes. But now I realize the reason why you keep eating even after you're full, and why I can't sleep no matter how tired I am is because we're suffering from the same thing."

Holmes sighed in exasperation. "And what, pray tell, would that be?"

"We're bored," Watson answered.

"What do you mean bored?" Holmes argued. "Since we arrived home, we've been busy doing lots of things."

"Like what?"

"Well," Holmes said, taking his time, "eating for one thing, sleeping for another."

"And what else?"

Holmes sat up in his bed. Watson recognized that movement, for each time Holmes had to think beyond dinner and going to bed, he sat back on his haunches and gazed upward either at the ceiling or the sky in deep concentration.

"Ah, I have it," Holmes said, eyes alert. "Going on walks with Millicent, sitting in Alfredo's lap, visiting Nonna and the Cellini's at their farm, and doing our business from time to time either on the grass, the flowers, or the canal ways of Venice."

"I suppose your right," Watson agreed. "But we 'aven't gone anywhere new lately, nor 'ave we been brought in to 'elp with the investigation of any new cases."

"I must agree, dear boy," Holmes said, pacing the floor in front of his pillow bed. "In fact, I think you have a very good point there."

"Yeah," Watson said with a yawn, "good point there."

"So let me strategize this out," Holmes continued, now extending his pacing to include the entire room. "It's far too early to disturb our mistress, so we'll wait until she awakens. Then after breakfast we'll nonchalantly mention that we'd like to go on vacation—someplace far away from home, but not too far should she feel uneasy about traveling so close to giving birth."

"Mmmmm," Watson murmured.

"I'll then attempt to rationalize the importance of us all taking a fabulous vacation, while you stare at her mournfully with those googly eyes of yours. How does that sound?"

No answer.

Holmes quickly pivoted ninety-degrees so as look back at Watson. "I said, how does that sound?"

Again no answer.

Holmes worriedly scampered across the floor back to where Watson lay. "I say, dear Watson. Have you not heard a single word I've been saying?"

Watson gave a quick snort. Then with his eyes shut tight and his little tongue peeking out from between his teeth, he purred ever so softly, "aahl limmmonnn."

The Case of the Magic Fluke

Chapter 1

"*Mamma mia,*" Millicent moaned from beneath the covers of her bed. "Alfredo, please tell me that's coffee I smell."

"One decaf cappuccino with added cream just for you, my darling," Alfredo crooned as he set the steaming cup of comfort on the end table next to his very pregnant wife before kissing the top of her brown-black hair. "How'd you sleep last night?"

"Oh," she moaned again. Then followed up with two hiccups and a rapid firing of sneezes. *Hiccup. Hiccup. Ah-choo, ah-choo, ah-choo, ah-choo, ah-choo!*

"Not well, thank you," she continued, accepting a fresh white linen handkerchief from Alfredo. "I swear, this baby sleeps all day, only to do some form of cross-fit or bikram yoga from the time I crawl into bed until morning. If I didn't know better, I'd say Baby Martolini enjoys either dancing the Macarena 'til the wee hours or hopping into a midnight mash pit somewhere between my sternum and my rib cage. And not simply once or twice, but all . . . night . . . long."

"I know, my darling," Alfredo said as he sat on the edge of the bed. "But it won't be long now before our little one will finally be here to keep us *both* up all night."

Millicent struggled to sit. Once settled, Alfredo handed over her cappuccino. "Here," he said, "this should make you feel as good as new."

"The only thing right now that would make me feel better is a long, gentle back massage," she whined between sips of coffee. "I tell you, Alfredo, I don't know how much more of this I can take."

Millicent Martolini, nee Winthrop, felt completely exhausted. And who wouldn't after the kind of year she'd had, she reasoned. Especially after having had the dangerous Vasilov Bugàr, along with his henchman, Luca "The Nose" Nasato, arrested and finally committed to house arrest. She'd then barely had time to breathe before rushing off to marry the love of her life, Alfredo, who just happened to be her ex-psychiatrist. You see, in addition to being very pregnant, Millicent was also aware that she suffered from what might easily be described as a multiple personality disorder. Or at least she did.

It all began four years ago when a ceiling tile in the guest bedroom of her friends, the Ricardous, became dislodged during a Los Angeles earthquake, striking her near the top left corner of her scalp—leaving her utterly disoriented and in need of professional help, which she received from a young intern working as an amnesia specialist for a London hospital at the time—her now husband, Dr. Alfredo Martolini.

She'd only consented to marry Alfredo after discovering with the help of his sister, Dr. Cecilia Cellini, who she truly was in spite of her history of amnesia—a byproduct of her long-standing personality disorder. Then soon after relocating with Alfredo to Berlin in order to solve the case of a kidnapped American goalkeeper, as they were commissioned to by FIFA, the Fédération Internationale de Football Association, she discovered she was pregnant. Needless to say, Millicent had earned a much-needed holiday.

And she wasn't the only one. Alfredo was as frazzled as she was, if not from flying here, there, and everywhere on assignment with his new wife, but from his concerns not only for Millicent's safety, but from his own self-doubts about his new job as a private investigator. Plus, he also shared the responsibility of taking care of Millicent's two therapy pugs, Holmes and Watson, who were doubtlessly self-sufficient and fiercely independent for lap dogs, but still as important to Millicent as she was to them.

All four were well aware of their responsibilities to each other, as well as to the head of FIFA's Security Council, Mr. Buckminster Smythe. So when it came time for her to suggest where after this long year she'd like the four of them to rest and recuperate, Millicent didn't need to think twice.

"Oh Alfredo," she said excitedly while jumping up and down in bed as best she could at eight months pregnant. "Let's spend a week at Bad Reichenhall. I haven't been there in nearly a year, and it used to be my favorite place to unwind and relax." Immediate she flashed onto a sensorial memory of her favorite masseuse—Helmut Hager and his famous magic fingers.

"Bad Reichenhall—that's the famous German spa just outside of Salzburg, sì?" Alfredo asked.

"*Ja wohl!*" Millicent blurted while clapping her hands. "The perfect place to let everything go as we soak in the mineral baths, submit to hours of reinvigorating massage—

"All right, all right," Alfredo said with a laugh, "you had me back at 'unwind'."

Holmes and Watson, having heard Millicent's squeals of excitement, left their beds and were now sauntering into their master and mistress's bedroom.

"We'll have such a marvelous time, Alfredo," Millicent said joyfully. "Not only must we take one of those long hikes through the Alps, but all four of us will be treated like royalty once we reach the spa. Then in Salzburg we can take in an opera—"

Alfredo's face noticeably perked up at the word *opera*.

"—or a concert, and visit all the exciting and wonderful Mozart museums, like his Geburtshaus."

"His *ge*-what?" Alfredo asked.

"The house where Mozart grew up," Millicent said, throwing herself into his arms. "Oh Alfredo, this holiday is the perfect thing for us. I just know it."

Holmes and Watson rolled their eyes. The last thing they wanted to do was go on a long and rigorous seventeen kilometer hike. Neither did they particularly want to go to an opera performance at the Salzburg Castle, nor even a concert in the middle of the town square. Yet as bored as they'd become, the two were hungering to go on another adventure, and knowing Millicent as well as they did by now, they were convinced that a marvelous adventure was most assuredly in their futures.

"If you get the tickets Alfredo," Millicent bargained as she waddled her way to her walk-in closet, "I'll go ahead and pack. The sooner we leave, the sooner our vacation can begin."

"I presume you want to leave today, sì?" Alfredo asked as she handed him her cappuccino before darting into their clothes closet.

"Sì," she yelled.

"And how much time do you need to get ready?"

Millicent suddenly appeared, her arms draped with several articles of clothing. "Oh, I suppose an hour is all. That is, if I can depend on your help, as well as that of Holmes and Watson."

"*Eccellente*," Alfredo remarked smilingly, knowing full well that Millicent could never be ready in that short amount of time.

"Do you think perhaps we should first make sure Mr. Smythe doesn't have something already planned for us, work-wise, that is?" she asked gingerly as she stood once again in the doorway.

Alfredo set down the now empty cup of java and circled his arms around her—tummy and all. "Now, darling," he said tenderly, "I distinctly remember that it was he who suggested we take some time off. We truly do need *una breve vacanza*, sì? I know I could use one, and I wouldn't be surprised if Holmes and Watson could use one as well. Besides, it won't be long now before we'll have our hands full with the baby."

"I suppose you're right," she said, snuggling her face against Alfredo's chest. "It's just that I've been working for Mr. Smythe for so long, it seems odd to suddenly be talking about holidays and spa treatments and babies."

Alfredo kissed her gently on the top of her head. "I can't wait to see you holding our little baby—*il nostro piccolo bambino*. You're going to be a beautiful mother, Millicent. There is no question in my mind."

Millicent looked up into Alfredo's sexy chocolate brown eyes and sighed. "And you'll make a wonderful father, too, Alfredo. Our little one's going to be one lucky child."

14

"*Assolutamente*," he answered gently and kissed her for all he was worth.

***

Holmes and Watson rolled their eyes once again, circled the floor where they'd been standing, plopped down onto their haunches, and covered their eyes with their paws.

"So, are we going on a 'oliday or not, 'olmes? I'm confused," Watson asked quietly.

Holmes cleared his throat, which he usually did whenever he had something important to say. "It's hard to say, but my guess is that we'll soon be on our way."

"Yeah," Watson echoed, "On our way."

He then suddenly lifted his paws from off his push face and whined with a look of fright in his googly eyes, "But I draw the line at going on a 'ike or spending the noyght at an op'ra."

***

When the two newlyweds finally came up for air, Alfredo stared at Millicent as she leaned against him, her sparking blue eyes half-closed, obviously relishing the taste of him on her lips.

"Well," she said, "I agree. We really do need a rest, but at the same time I want everything here at the house ready for the baby before we leave. Otherwise, I'm afraid I won't be able to fully enjoy myself for worry about what needs to be done."

"And what's so important that needs to be done?" he asked, feigning ignorance.

"What needs to be done?" Millicent asked anxiously. "Why, we have to put together the baby crib, the matching chest of drawers, the changing table, the rocking chair, the playpen . . . ."

Alfredo watched with a smirk on his face as Millicent began to pace up and down the hallway. "—the bottle sterilizer, the recipe for the formula, and the baby monitors in both the baby's room and ours . . . ."

The faster the wheels spun in her brain, the faster she waddled, her words cascading like a runaway train.

"And I have to sort all the fabulous baby clothes I've already purchased in every size from newborn up to three years old. Of course, that includes socks, shoes, hats, coats, diapers, undershirts, pajamas, and I think I even bought a pair of roller skates," she rattled on, counting her fingers.

Alfredo immediately broke out into laughter, swept away by Millicent's spirited enthusiasm.

"Look," she continued, "I know it's asking a lot, but I think it would be super nice before the baby comes if we could have some time together. Our honeymoon was wonderful, and I'll never forget it. But it happened in the middle of winter. And to be quite honest, walking around in a lovely little sundress across the *Residenzplatz* in midtown Salzburg seems like the perfect way to celebrate this our very first year together."

"All right Millicent, you've talked me into it," Alfredo said with a hug. "I'll call Mr. Smythe and make sure we're actually free to take the kind of holiday we truly want. If he gives us the go-ahead, then we're out of here."

"You mean, as soon as we get everything put together?" she asked carefully.

"Sì, Signora Martolini, as soon as everything is assembled," he said, and kissed her again for the third time.

Millicent immediately rushed off to pack and take care of the things she needed to take care of—whatever that was—usually her hair rollers, makeup, different pairs of socks, shoes to match every outfit, of course, and an emergency overnight bag just in case she'd have to make a quick stop at a hospital in time to have the baby.

In the meantime, Alfredo picked up the dogs' leads, clipped them to the collars of both Holmes and Watson, grabbed his mobile, and took the boys out for a much needed stroll. The temperature in Venice was already moving toward the heat of summer. And even though a lovely breeze wafted in from the Adriatic, across Saint Marco's Square, and over the Accademia Bridge to where their home lay, Alfredo was convinced that it would be beyond paradise to stay for the hottest part of the summer in the temperate mountain town of Salzburg, Austria.

It had been such a long time since he'd gone to any kind of concert or opera, and Lord knows he loved the opera. Especially Italian opera. Verdi, Puccini, Donizetti—those were his kind of composers. And, of course, Mozart. There was always something quite wonderful about Mozart. And, although he'd always heard good things about Salzburg, he'd never been, in spite of his good intentions. He'd either been too busy with clients, or taking care of his aging mother Emilia, or chasing after Millicent.

"When again is the baby due?" Alfredo asked out loud to himself.

Holmes again cleared his throat and immediately looked up at his master. "Excuse me sir," he said in his most formal tone of voice, "but I believe the baby is due sometime in September, if my calculations are correct."

Alfredo knew that Holmes was probably speaking to him, but, damn—even though they'd been together now going on the fourth of fifth year, somewhere in there—for the life of him, Alfredo had no idea what Holmes was saying. Yet both dogs seemed nonetheless happy, trotting along the canal streets of Venice as if they owned them—and with Alfredo following close behind, taking the time to phone Mr. Smythe as the boys did their business.

The phone on the other end rang but twice before being answered. "FIFA headquarters, Madeleine Bay speaking."

"Hello Madeleine," Alfredo greeted. "Is Mr. Smythe available?"

"Just a moment, I'll check." Madeleine was Mr. Smythe's executive assistant. She took her job quite seriously and never let a phone call go through unless it was absolutely imperative. Unfortunately, she seldom believed the calls from Millicent or Alfredo were as important as they actually were.

After a long pause, she returned to the phone. "He'll be right with you," she said, and for a second time immediately put Alfredo's call on hold.

The intercom music on the telephone call-waiting was an assortment of different instrumental and vocal selections especially written for either the upcoming World Cup or Euro Cup games. Those tournaments alternated every two years, so the music was one way to keep account of where one was in the calendar of events. Alfredo couldn't help but grin as he thought of how easily Millicent even still got dates and appointments messed up. He was sure the behavior had much to do with her years of dealing with the side effects of her multiple personality disorder. Yet now that she was at last well, Alfredo merely chalked up her forgetfulness to who she was—quirks and all.

At last Mr. Smythe picked up his phone. "Buckminster Smythe here. What can I do for you Alfredo?"

"*Buona pomeriggio*, Mr. Smythe. I hope you don't mind, but I thought I'd give you a quick call to make sure Millicent and I are allowed to go on a little family vacation over the next few weeks. Before the baby comes."

The Case of the Magic Fluke

"Ah, Alfredo. It's so good of you to call. Of course, that sounds wonderful, but let me double check." Alfredo could hear papers rapidly shuffling in the background. "As far as I can tell," Mr. Smythe continued, "we're free at this moment from any impending cases."

"You're sure?"

"Yes, that's correct. I don't see anything on the calendar. And I can't think of anything right off the top of my head, but if something should come up, is there someplace where I can get a hold of you? Will Holmes and Watson be traveling with you?"

"Millicent talked me into traveling to Salzburg and perhaps Bad Reichenhall," Alfredo answered. "And you know Millicent. She doesn't go anywhere without Holmes and Watson in tow."

"Well, it's a good thing she does," Mr. Smythe reflected. "I don't know how many times that woman has gotten herself into trouble. Why, if it were not for those two pugs, she surely by now would be . . . well, we don't even want to think about that, do we?"

"No sir, we don't," Alfredo answered firmly. "I sometimes wish Millicent understood how vulnerable she is, especially now that she's within days of having our baby."

"Is she really that far along?" Mr. Smith asked. "Heavens, time travels fast."

"Yes, and we're both so very excited," Alfredo said, his voice noticeably cheering up.

"And do you know as of yet if you're having a boy or girl?" Mr. Smythe knew his wife Sabrina would want to know all the details once he got home and told her of his conversation with Alfredo.

"Yes, absolutely," Alfredo said with a chuckle. "Last I heard, we're having either a boy or a girl."

"Ah, that's very good news," Mr. Smythe guffawed. "I'm so glad that you've determined at this point that you're not having a third canine assistant."

"*Mio Dio*," Alfredo said, laughing even louder. "Can you imagine? Our hands are already more than full with Holmes and Watson, thank you. Adding a third pug would just about break our mental health bank, forcing us to lose what little sanity we have left?"

"Speaking of which," Mr. Smythe added, "how has Millicent's mental state been these last few weeks? Has she had any recent premonitions, visions, or strange imaginings that we here at FIFA should know about?"

"You mean, has she forgotten who she is, or where she is, or what it is she's supposed to be doing?"

"Yes, exactly."

"I don't think so," Alfredo answered. "Honestly, as far as I can tell she's our Millicent, yet for whatever reason she hasn't had one of her episodes in a very long time."

"Do you think that's a good thing or a bad thing given her mental state?"

Alfredo noted the obvious concern in Mr. Smythe's voice. "With regard to her general health, I'd say it's a good thing. Those trances take a great deal out of her, sometime forcing her to go to bed soon after and sleep for three or four days."

"I wondered as much," Mr. Smythe said.

"However, it's been her superpower, without which I sometimes doubt if she'll ever be able to do the kind of top notch detective work she's already accomplished and been known for in the past. "

"So, you think her talent for criminal investigation is linked to her multiple personality disorder?"

Alfredo swiped his hair back from off his forehead and held his palm there as he thought hard about how to answer the retired Scotland Yard detective. "I can honestly say that I'm not sure one way or another. But it concerns me, especially now that she's about to have this baby."

"Answer me this, Alfredo," Mr. Smythe pressed. "Does she still talk to Holmes and Watson as if they understand her every word?"

"Oh, sì," Alfredo chortled, "and she still listens to every bark they answer in return. No, the three of them still have lengthy conversations, which I am getting used to but still unable to entirely understand."

Alfredo glanced down at his two canine assistants, who sat patiently staring up at him with looks of obvious worry on each of their muzzles.

"I see," Mr. Smythe answered. "Well, let's keep this situation between us for now. Millicent obviously still has some remnants of psychosis left in her personality, but as long as she feels well and can do her work, we'll let it go for now."

"I'm certain Millicent is making great strides in her recovery," Alfredo said, not only for Mr. Smythe's benefit, but for Holmes's and Watson's as well. "She's happily excited about becoming a new mother and will likewise be elated to hear that we have your okay to enjoy a short holiday before the baby comes."

"No matter what, Alfredo, enjoy yourselves," Mr. Smythe added. "And keep me posted if anything should come up concerning Millicent's continued health."

"Will do, Mr. Smythe, and thank you so very much for all you've done to make Millicent feel loved and needed. She enjoys working for FIFA, and respects you a great deal."

"And I appreciate you and Millicent as well, Alfredo," Mr. Smythe said with a hitch in his voice. "Give her my love, and an extra amaretto biscotti to Holmes and Watson from me as well. Ciao, Alfredo."

"Ciao," he answered and then closed his phone to slip it back into his shirt pocket. "Don't worry about Millicent, boys," he said as he crouched down to their eye level, scratching each of them behind their ears. "Mr.

Smythe and I are keeping a close eye on her, for she means as much to us as she does to you. *Capire?*"

Holmes and Watson immediately charged Alfredo's legs, nearly knocking him over with their exuberant jumps, barks, and licks. He couldn't, of course, be sure if they fully understood what he'd said or not, but from the look of things, he had good reason to hope.

Chapter 2

Five hours later Millicent and Alfredo, along with Holmes and Watson, found themselves in a taxi headed for the Marco Polo airport. Normally they would not have splurged for a cab, but no way would Alfredo and the boys' two suitcases along with Millicent's four fit in Alfredo's Maserati, and so they had no other choice but to pay the big bucks. Besides, they were running late as it was, which was no surprise to Alfredo, since Millicent even before she was pregnant always seemed to be chasing the clock.

Luckily, however, the flight had barely begun its boarding process when the entourage stampeded across the terminal proper. And thanks to Alfredo's much admired multi-tasking ability—one of his many talents Millicent absolutely loved and depended upon—within minutes their luggage was checked in, their tickets stamped, and their collective arses wedged into their assigned seats.

"Perhaps you were right, Alfredo," Millicent said as she wiggled around in an attempt to stretch out her shoulders and back. "We should have taken Mr. Smythe up on his offer to fly us to Salzburg via the company jet."

Alfredo placed the last piece of carryon luggage in the compartment above Millicent's head. "I agree it would have made the trip a bit easier for us," he said, seating himself across the aisle. "Yet since we are not on assignment but rather traveling for our own enjoyment, I think flying commercial as we are was the better choice."

"I suppose you're right, as usual," she admitted, "but try saying that to my poor back." Immediately Holmes and Watson, seated on either side of her, cuddled against their mistress, doing their best to give her what comfort they could.

"I know, darling. I'm sorry. The good news, though, is that we'll be landing in Salzburg in barely over an hour. And Mr. Smythe has already booked us into a lovely hotel located on the river, close to the old part of the city, so we'll be able to see all the sights whenever we want and without having to walk too far."

Suddenly Millicent's two canine assistants perked up. Holmes made a noise much like an old man clearing his throat, and Watson let out a strangely frightening little howl.

"See," said Millicent giggling, "even the boys are happy to hear that."

***

Which was true. Holmes and Watson both enjoyed exploring new places as well as revisiting old haunts. But hiking monotonously up and down steep mountain trails was not to be tolerated, particularly by Watson.

"Did ya 'ear that, 'olmes? Maybe we won't 'ave to go 'iking after all," he yipped gleefully.

"Yes, I heard," he answered. "As you well know, nothing is wrong with my hearing."

"Although a lit'uhl exercise wouldn't 'urt you," Watson added with a snort. "Looks to me like you've gained some since moving to Venice."

"That does it," Holmes announced as he quickly leapt over Millicent and into Watson's seat. "For your information, I am not fat. I'm merely big boned. That's all."

For emphasis, Holmes began to lick the insides of Watson's ears with a ferocity that bordered on the maniacal.

"Ouch, 'olmes. That 'urts," he said, cowering away.

"Rubbish," Holmes said with a growl. "I'm not hurting you in any way whatsoever. I'm merely cleaning your ears and reminding you of who's boss. And I'm waiting for an apology."

Watson wasn't altogether sure that it was only his ears and not also his brain that was getting a good once over. "All right," he said at last, "I'm sorry I said anything about your weight, 'olmes."

"That's better," Holmes said, once again crossing over Millicent's lap while heading back to his seat.

"I wouldn't 'ave said anything 'ad I known you were in such a shirty mood," Watson said, obviously pushing his luck.

"I'm only get into a shirty mood when you find occasion to make those kinds of disparaging comments concerning my waistline."

Watson thought about what Holmes had said as he watched his brother curl back up onto his seat. Finally, after another thirty seconds or so he said softly for only Holmes to hear, "Thanks for cleaning my ears, 'olmes. And I promise not to say another word about your recent weight gain for the rest our 'oliday, no matter 'ow much I want to."

Too tired to say or do anything, Holmes merely closed his eyes and slept the rest of the flight.

***

Millicent was more than familiar with the Salzburg airport. Over the last four years she'd traveled to Bad Reichenhall and stayed at the lovely German resort more than once. In fact, if the truth were known, she'd stayed there at least a dozen times or more. It was her favorite place to relax, unwind, and forget about the difficulties and disappointments of the day. On this particular day she was hoping to forget all about her lower back and swollen ankles.

Cunigunda *Valentine*

As soon as the plane landed, Millicent and the pugs immediately retrieved their suitcases from baggage claim, while Alfredo picked up the rental car Mr. Smythe had reserved for them. Once he'd placed their few carry-on items in the boot, Alfredo got in and following the signage, drove to where Millicent and the boys were waiting. Sure enough, there sat Millicent along with Holmes and Watson on top of the four huge remaining suitcases, so he pulled the car up as close to the curb as possible.

Now, it didn't take a genius to realize that the car was far too small for the four of them, plus their luggage, plus Millicent's rather large baby bump, which is probably why Watson was the first to speak.

"If you don't mind, Millicent," he began, "I'd rather us take a taxi."

"Rubbish," Holmes blurted, "I'm sure we'll all fit if we merely hold our breath. Besides, a taxi, though very nice, is still quite expensive."

Realizing that Alfredo more than likely wasn't catching a word the two pugs were saying, Millicent took over the conversation.

"Do you think we'll be able to all fit in this car, Alfredo?" she asked. "It seems to me to be a bit on the small side."

"Of course, we'll all fit," he answered. "After all, I'm Italian, and we Italians know how to pack a car. Don't you worry yourself darling."

"If you say so, dear," she answered carefully.

And he was right. For within twenty minutes Alfredo had organized everything to where it fit like a Fratelli Orsini leather glove. Two large

29

suitcases took over the boot, with the other two straddling the back seat. The two smaller pieces of luggage sat on the back seat floor with Holmes curled up on the top of one and Watson on the other. Millicent sat in the passenger seat, holding on to the seat belt as best she could since it was too short to go completely around her tummy, and Alfredo sat behind the wheel with his wife's handbag wedged between his legs.

"See," he said proudly, "what did I tell you, eh? *Calza come un guanto!*"

"Yeah," whispered Watson to Holmes, "like a glove."

***

In no time at all Alfredo pulled the rental car up to the address of the hotel Mr. Smythe had reserved for them. As soon as the car stopped, all four passengers sat silent for a moment and stared at the edifice before them.

Millicent didn't exactly know what she was expecting, but what stood before her wasn't even on the map of her imagination. "Alfredo, do you see what I see?"

"I believe so," he said as gobsmacked as she.

"Are you sure you have the correct address? Let me see your phone and I'll double check the email from Mr. Smythe," she demanded, grabbing the phone from Alfredo's hand.

Indeed the address and picture of the hotel on the phone were identical to what they were all staring at through the windshield.

"Well, I'll be," she said at last. "Blimey, if Mr. Smythe didn't reserve for us a room at a bleedin' five star hotel. And it's absolutely stunning."

"Huzzah," both boys exclaimed while jumping up and down in the back of the car.

"I truly am at a loss of words," Alfredo admitted, "but at the same time rather delighted. How about you, Millicent?"

She looked over at Alfredo and gave him a wink. "Let's all go in and check it out. I can hardly wait to see our room," she said as she squeezed herself out the door. "Besides, I have to use the loo. Again."

Alfredo chuckled. "Of course, darling, I'm rather curious myself." He then leashed up Holmes and Watson as a precaution and led them toward the hotel office. The last thing they needed was for Watson to relieve himself in the lobby, as he was wont to do.

As soon as the four of them entered the building, Millicent, astounded by its abject beauty, took Alfredo's hand so as to steady herself should she feel faint.

"I don't think I've ever been is such a beautiful place as this, Alfredo," she whispered. "I feel as if I'm royalty, or at the very least, very, very rich."

"You are royalty, my love," Alfredo said as he nuzzled Millicent's neck. "You are my queen for now and always."

"And you are my prince, Alfredo," she answered before giving him a kiss on his cheek.

The Case of the Magic Fluke

Suddenly a man stood up from behind the registration counter, causing them both to jump. "May I help you?" he asked.

"Yes, thank you," Millicent said. "Where is your ladies room located?" Millicent hoped she hadn't already had an accident. The concierge pointed to Millicent's right, while Alfredo identified himself.

"*Buongiorno*," Alfredo greeted as Millicent ran to where she had been directed. "I am Alfredo Martolini, and I believe Mr. Smythe from FIFA headquarters already called in our reservation. And who might you be?"

"Ah," the man said, seeing the name *Martolini* on his computer screen. "I am your concierge, Reinhardt Rauscher. And I do indeed see you have a prepaid reservation for our junior suite during the following two weeks here at our luxurious and historic hotel."

"*Eccellente*," Alfredo said. "And is there someone who could take our luggage up to our room?"

"Of course," said the concierge. "I will take care of that for you. And while I do, please take care of your pets."

"My *what*?"

"I assume that's your dog over there to the left, relieving himself in the potted plant. And also the chubbier one to the right, who looks as though he's helping himself to the plate of freshly baked biscuits on the table by the espresso machine."

"*O, per l'amor del cielo*," Alfredo sputtered. It wasn't until now that he realized that neither he nor Millicent had a handle on the boys' leash. "I am so sorry, Signor Rauscher. *Ti prego, perdonami.* Please forgive me. I'll fetch them right this minute."

"Please do so, Herr Martolini," the concierge said firmly. "Then return here to the desk so that you may sign our registration book and pick up the keys to your suite."

"Holmes. Watson. Both of you come here right this minute," Alfredo ordered. "Watson, you know better than to go potty indoors, particularly in a public space."

He then took a hold of Watson's leash and marched him over to where Holmes was hiding behind a chair, still munching on what was left of the biscuits.

"And you, Holmes," Alfredo retorted as he leashed up the canine thief. "You know you're not supposed to run away and indulge in *biscotti*, especially when they are not yours to eat."

"Yeah, chubby," Watson added with a snicker, which set Holmes off into a circular chase around Alfredo's legs, sending him to the floor.

It was then that Millicent appeared. Immediately her smile of contentment was altered into one of horror. "What in the world is going on here?" she asked the boys." And why is it you're groveling on the floor, Alfredo?"

"I'm not groveling, Millicent," Alfredo said impatiently. "I'm trying my best to rein in these two hooligans, but as you can see, I'm not doing a very good job of it."

Holmes and Watson lay still, their eyes covered by their front paws, waiting for their punishment. But all Millicent could do was laugh. "You three are the silliest looking creatures I've ever had the pleasure of enjoying. Now, let's all quit fooling around, that includes you too Alfredo, and check out our accommodation. I want to freshen up from our trip, and I'm sure you three do as well."

***

By the time they made it to their room, the four were at last enjoying each other's company. Watson kept his teasing remarks to himself, Holmes refrained from telling the little imp what to do, and Alfredo blew off his embarrassment by chuckling at the ridiculousness of it all. As requested, their entire luggage had made it to their suite, which was indeed a beautiful accommodation. Located on the third floor, this lovely suite stood complete with a king size bed, a small sitting area with a large TV, and a cute little round table situated just the other side of the balcony overlooking the Salzach River.

Thoroughly satisfied, Millicent quickly set about unpacking and organizing their belongings. In no time she'd finished her task and was ready to either take a nap or eat a snack. Instead, she remembered what it was she wanted to do first thing she arrived.

"Alfredo," she said, "would you mind terribly if I went and got a massage before dinner? Perhaps you and the boys would like to roam about the city for a bit, take in some sites, get the lay of the land. I promise I won't be very long."

Millicent, who had an impossible time trying to nap on the plane, decided that before any more time went by she wanted to go see her old friend Helmut for a massage.

"That sounds wonderful, darling," Alfredo said. "Holmes and Watson and I are more than happy to give you the afternoon as long as we can entertain you this evening."

"Oh, thank you, Alfredo. Grazie," she said, kissing him sweetly. "I promise I won't be more than an hour, Perhaps we can go out someplace fun for dinner tonight."

As soon as she said the word *dinner*, Millicent noticed Holmes and Watson's ears once again perked up, causing her to smile in spite of her aching back.

"Don't worry about us, *mia cara*," Alfredo said. "We'll be fine. You take your time and get the massage you want. The boys and I might have a small snack in the meantime, but don't you fret. We won't spoil our appetites."

Again Millicent kissed Alfredo—this time for all she was worth—then walked over to the sofa where Holmes and Watson lay, scratched them both behind their ears, and said goodbye. Before she could say "Bob's your uncle," she was in the car ready to head toward Bad Reichenhall.

The Case of the Magic Fluke

First, though, she felt she should call the resort to make sure Helmut would be available for her much needed appointment. Luckily his number was still in her mobile.

"Hallo," Millicent said once her call was picked up. "This is Millicent Winthrop. I was wondering if there might be an opportunity for me to see Helmut this afternoon. You see, I'm very pregnant, my back is killing me, and I feel like my legs are the size of an elephant's."

"Are you speaking of Helmut Hager?" the voice over the phone asked.

"Yes Helmut Hager," she said, rolling her eyes. *What other Helmut is there?* "Is he available?"

"Luckily for you, Herr Hager has a cancellation beginning in fifteen minutes. Do you think you could make it on time to take his next hour and a half?"

"I'll be there in a shake," Millicent said. And with that she threw her phone into her tote, put both hands on the steering wheel, and let her foot ease into the gas pedal. Normally it took about 30 minutes to get from Salzburg to Bad Reichenhall, especially in traffic, but today the road was open with nary a car in sight. Within seconds Millicent was flying down the highway in anticipation for the massage of her dreams.

Chapter 3

It had turned out to be a beautiful day in Salzburg. Many locals and tourists were taking advantage of the warmth of the sun, so like them Alfredo harnessed up the boys and the three of them took a much needed walk. They started out by first crossing the river, which led them to the more historic and touristy part of the city. As they approached the main square, the *Residenzplatz*, many exquisite sights and tempting smells captured their senses.

"Oim 'ungry," Watson whined. "When are we gonna stop and 'ave a couple bangers and mash, or a 'elping of spotted dick, or perhaps an eel pie?"

"Dear boy," Holmes answered, "for your information we're not in England at the moment, we're in Austria—the home of *erdäpfelgulasch*,

37

käsespätzle, and *der Wiener würstchen.*"

"Wha—"

"Potato and apple gulasch, macaroni and cheese, and the ever popular cocktail wiener—Austrian style." Holmes liked to stay culturally informed.

"Nah," Watson answered frowning, "I want something sweet and fresh baked, like those biscuits you ate at the 'otel, which by the way you refused to share."

"For your information, Watson, there truly weren't enough biscuits to share. One or two, that's it."

"I just wanted one," Watson replied.

"Hey, you two," Alfredo interrupted, "it sounds to me as if you're quarreling about something. And we can't have that, you know."

Holmes and Watson both stopped where they were at and hung their heads, their eyes fixed on the pavement in front of them.

"We're finally on holiday, which means we are supposed to have fun and be extra nice to each other. *Capisci?*"

Slowly both dogs looked up at him with sad googly eyes, and Alfredo immediately felt bad for having to scold them. "Okay, enough said. Let's go find us something delicious to eat, sì?"

As fate would have it, the three hadn't walked more than a few paces when they were face to face with a bake shop whose window was jammed full of sweets of every variety. Biscuits, tarts, cakes, pies, and an assortment of strudels—apricot, peach, blueberry, raspberry, and, of course, apple.

Alfredo had his usual issue with deciding which dessert to purchase, so he simply bought several of each item the *Bäckerei* offered, and with Holmes and Watson's complete approval. He and the boys then continued their stroll until they found the perfect table for three at a nearby outdoor café. There they all sat patiently as Alfredo ordered a cappuccino for himself and two small bowls of water for each of the pugs. And not until his coffee arrived did he begin to divide the pasties between them.

"This tastes marvelous," Watson said with his mouth stuffed full.

"Don't talk with your mouth full, Watson," Holmes admonished. "It's not polite."

"But I can't 'elp it," Watson replied. "I'm too 'ungry to be polite."

Holmes rolled his eyes and continued munching delicately on the lovely Linzertorte set before him. Watson in the meantime devoured his selections as quickly as Alfredo could set them down. It didn't take but just a few minutes and Holmes was snoring, lost in the sugar-hazed dream, chasing butterflies and bees.

Watson however did not fare as well, as he now lay directly on his back moaning with all four of his legs straight up.

"What's the matter Watson," Alfredo asked. "Did you eat too many sweets too quickly?" All Watson could do was moan.

And so for some length of time Alfredo's two canine assistants stationed themselves next to his feet, a snore from Holmes alternating between each of Watson's moans.

***

"Ah, Helmut," Millicent sighed, "how I have missed your touch so very much."

"*Ja Fräulein*," Helmut said in agreement. "I mean, Frau Martolini. I have missed you as well."

"I especially love this new therapy bed of yours," she said dreamily with her eyes closed. "Whatever made you think to design a bed with a hole in the middle of it?"

"Oh, I did that purposely, Millicent dear," Helmut said, squeezing the knots out of her lower back. "Many a pregnant woman finds she has a longing to lie on her stomach, but because of the baby, it's impossible. But, with a hole in the bed, insert baby bump, and *voilà*, the pregnant woman is now laying on her stomach and as happy as a pig in pudding."

"You're a genius, Helmut," Millicent moaned. "And whatever it is you're doing right now, please keep doing it. I haven't felt this *wunderbar* since the last time I was here."

"*Ja Fräulein*," Helmut answered. "I always try to do my best."

Within minutes a soft snore was heard coming from underneath the massage table. Millicent was fast asleep and doing so more soundly than she had in a long time.

***

After what in the long run tended to be a nice nap under the adept fingers of Helmut Hager, Millicent felt rejuvenated and ready for the rest of the evening. Remarkably, her back felt miraculously relieved, and her legs had never before been thinner at the ankles, nor more shapely at the top of the calves.

"I'm back," she said as she entered the suite.

Nothing.

"Hallo, is anyone here?" she tried again.

Alfredo along with Holmes and Watson would've answered her back, but they all three were fast asleep—Alfredo in the middle of the king size bed with Holmes and Watson snuggled against him.

Millicent had to giggle for she really wasn't sure who looked cuter, Alfredo or her two canine assistants. In either case she decided to go ahead and take a quick shower. She knew it wouldn't be long before she'd start getting hungry again, and she didn't want to be the one to hold the four of them up from going out for a lovely evening's meal.

Yet before entering the sumptuous marble-encased bathroom, Millicent's espied something that looked a little like an apple strudel sitting on a plate on the small dining table with her name on a card next to it.

Quietly but swiftly she made her way over to the welcoming dessert. She then picked up the note and read the following:

The Case of the Magic Fluke

To dear sweet Millicent, whom we all love,

something for your enjoyment that's as delicious as you are.

It was signed *Alfredo*, but below his name she noticed two sets of paw prints drawn on it as well. She was so taken aback by the sweetness of the note, she at once teared up. "These pregnancy hormones are turning me into one major crybaby," she whispered to herself.

Not wanting to spoil her dinner, Millicent broke off a small piece of the strudel and allowed the buttery confection to melt in her mouth. She then wiped her eyes, blew her nose, and made her way into the shower. By the time she got out, Alfredo and the boys were up and ready to ferry off to a much-awaited-for dinner.

***

Upon Alfredo's suggestion, Millicent and crew decided to have dinner at the hotel's impressive Michelin star restaurant. Once again, Mr. Smythe had covered the cost of the meal as a special thanks for their incomparable service to FIFA. All they had to do was come up with the gratuity, which in itself cost more than what they usually spent on an entire meal. But it was worth it. In fact, as far as Millicent was concerned, it was just right. Even Watson acted the perfect gentleman.

Holmes and Watson shared an entrée of stuffed trout, which they gulped down in two minutes flat. Alfredo had the *Tafelspitz*, which basically was tender boiled beef with root vegetables, a true Austrian specialty. And

Millicent ended up ordering the paprika chicken with potato dumplings. Even though they were all four stuffed to the gills, they decided to also share a couple of desserts—the hotel's famous *Sachertorte*, a superlative chocolate gateau, and the region's *pièce de résistance*, the *Salzburger Nockerl*, a fluffy dessert made primarily from egg whites baked in the shape of three snow-capped mountains.

"I'm so full I can hardly move," Millicent said as she pried herself out of her chair.

"Not so fast, darling," Alfredo interrupted. "While the boys and I were out scouting the city, we decided to bring you back a surprise."

"Oh, yes. I had a bite of it before my shower," she said. "And what a lovely surprise it was. You know how much I enjoy a good strudel."

Holmes and Watson both chuckled, or at least to Alfredo's ears, it sounded like chuckling. Pug style.

"Uhm, yes, the strudel," he said, smiling. "But also I have an even better surprise."

"Really?" Millicent in her excitement momentarily forgot all about her full tummy and started to clap her hands and wiggle in her chair. "This is so much fun. Tell me. What have you three cooked up?"

Holmes sat up in his chair and barked while Watson placed his front paws on the table in front of him and howled.

"I bought us all tickets for tonight's performance of Mozart's *The*

The Case of the Magic Fluke

Magic Flute at the Salzburger Marionettentheater.

"You didn't," she screamed for joy.

"I did," he said, standing up from the table.

"Oh, Alfredo. How brilliant! I've always wanted to see a performance there. And of my favorite Mozart opera, too," she said, this time escaping her chair in order to give Alfredo a big hug and kiss.

"But we'll have to get going as the performance begins soon," he said.

"Oh, my. Well, yes, of course," she said. "And since we're going to be some time at the theater, it's probably best we walk there and give the boys a chance to do their business."

"Of course, *mia cara*. I'll leash up the boys."

"Also, I'm afraid I must use the restroom as well, Alfredo," she added. "I swear my bladder these days is the size of a walnut."

Holmes and Watson looked at each other for a brief moment and then up at their mistress.

"So what's wrong with 'aving a bladder the size of a walnut?" Watson asked Holmes in a whisper. "That's all I've ever 'ad to work with."

"Which is probably why you pee every three minutes," Holmes said sarcastically.

"Well," Watson said, "a pug 'as to do what a pug 'as to do."

Holmes merely chortled. "Yes, your right, Watson. And likewise a pregnant Millicent must do whatever a pregnant Millicent has to do."

***

It wasn't far to the theater from where they were. Yet by the time they got there, they were already a few minutes late, and so had to wait until the usher gave them permission to go to their seats, which happened to be near the very front of the stage and in the middle of a very crowded row.

At the first lull of the action, the usher motioned for them to follow her in order to be seated. Now, they'd just been escorted to their seats when a large puppet in the shape of a very long snake entered onto the marionette stage. Before Millicent or Alfredo could stop him, Watson leapt out of Millicent's arms and made a dash toward the stage, snarling and barking all the way.

"Watson, no," Holmes yipped, but it was too late. Within seconds Watson had the puppet in his craw and was violently shaking the monster to what he hoped was his demise.

"Watson, stop. Come here this instant. Bad dog," Millicent shouted as she, too, toppled onto the stage, chasing Watson before he'd completely destroyed the marionette. Unfortunately, Watson didn't stop, at least not until he had completely tangled up the strings of the different marionettes playing the roles of Tamino, Papageno, and such.

The production came to a standstill, but not for any other reason but the audience's laughter. By the time Millicent got both dogs back in their seats, the audience was howling. From the look on her face, Millicent could guess that the house manager was ready to throw them all out on their ears. Yet as soon as the audience saw what they assumed was the intention of the already frazzled house manager, they began to boo.

"Let them stay! Let them stay!" they chanted. And the house manager had no other recourse but to hold her temper in check while giving Millicent and company a good scolding. Within minutes the audience had settled down and the marionettes restarted their performance—minus the serpent puppet, of course.

Alfredo leaned over and whispered into Millicent's ear. "I'm surprised they let us stay. Aren't you?"

"I suppose so," she answered. "Even though Watson stopped the performance, it seemed to me that the audience really didn't mind, just the actors and the people in charge."

"Well, leave it to Watson," Alfredo chuckled. "If it's not one thing with that *piccolo carlini*, it's another."

"I think we're all settled down now," Millicent said," so let's forget what happened and try to enjoy the rest of the act."

***

"Bugger all," Holmes said, exasperatingly. "What were you thinking, Watson?"

"I couldn't 'elp it, 'olmes. I saw that 'umongous snake attacking the puppet, and something inside of me told me to pounce on it and give it what for."

"Pounce on it, you did," Holmes remarked. In fact, you destroyed that marionette so utterly, I doubt they'll be able to put it back together any time soon."

"Yeah, anytime soon," Watson agreed.

"Now, try to behave yourself for the rest of the performance. And if you can't do that," Holmes added, "then shut your eyes and keep them shut until I tell you it's safe to open them."

"All right 'olmes," Watson agreed. "Nothing will cause me to run up onto the stage the rest of the evening."

"Promise?"

"Yeah," Watson avowed, "I promise."

***

It wasn't but a half hour later, just before intermission, when once again Watson's eyes flew open as he sat up on his haunches atop his seat.

"Shh, quiet Watson," Millicent ordered, "sit back down and stop your howling."

Holmes, who'd been dozing on his seat since the serpent incident, immediately woke upon hearing Millicent's words.

"Now what's going on with Watson?" Alfredo whispered to Millicent. "Do you think he's hungry? Should I take him outside?"

Millicent peaked over at the little rascal. "I'm sure he's all right,

Alfredo." Just then the sound of a flute scurrying up part of major scale caught everyone's attention.

"Oh dear," Millicent said, "I think Watson is somehow attracted to that magic flute sound the character of Tamino is supposed to be making."

"Ah sì," Alfredo said, "the one the three ladies have just given him."

"Exactly," she agreed. Again the character of Tamino blew on his flute, this time calling forth all the strange and beautiful animals of the forest where he'd been wandering for some time. Again he sounded his flute. And again.

That was all Watson needed for him to once again fly out of his chair and join the marionette performance, wild animals and all. This time Millicent could not catch him, nor could Holmes or Alfredo. He was in trouble but so were they all—particularly since this time the audience was neither patient nor understanding.

It took three ushers and the house manager along with Millicent, Alfredo, and Holmes to capture the little pug and bring him under their control.

"Madam," the house manager said at last catching up to them, "I'm afraid I'm going to have to ask you and your company to leave."

"Oh dear," Millicent said between three sneezes and four hiccups. "We're terribly sorry. I had no idea Watson would react like that again. Normally he's a very good boy, so I don't know what's got into them.

Maybe it's something he ate."

Holmes merely rolled his eyes as Alfredo leashed up both he and Watson. As soon as they all hit the sidewalk, Millicent began to giggle.

"Oi'm sorry Millicent," Watson said as soon as his paws hit the pavement.

"Goodness," she said, "you've no reason to be sorry. Why, I don't remember when I've had more fun at an opera performance than I've had this evening."

Alfredo joined her laughter. "Me neither," he agreed.

The sun was barely beginning to set, giving the family of four just enough light to enjoy their pleasant walk back to the hotel.

Chapter 4

The next morning found Millicent and Alfredo taking Holmes and Watson out for an early morning stroll. As usual, the boys were hungry. And Alfredo without his morning cappuccino was far too crabby to go without. Thus the four of them trotted across a different bridge from yesterday to find something yummy to eat in the city.

Normally, Millicent would   make for herself a working woman's breakfast, complete with eggs, pancakes or waffles, toast or hash browns, and either sausage or bacon. Still feeling the results from last night's dinner, she decided this morning to forgo breakfast and instead share a cappuccino with Alfredo. Her stomach wasn't completely empty, however, as she did polish off what was left of the strudel when she got up in the middle of the night to use the loo.

Cunigunda *Valentine*

Alfredo with leash in hand allowed Holmes and Watson to lead the way to the same outdoor cafe and bakery they'd been at yesterday afternoon. Without slowing down for a second, the four hungry vacationers made a beeline for the pastry case, where everything from croissants to pretzels, strudels to tortes, and jelly donuts to Danishes lay decoratively before them.

"Do you see anything you might like, Millicent?" Alfredo asked. "I realize this isn't your usual bill of fare, but I promise I'll make it up to you *a pranzo*—at lunchtime."

Millicent scanned the dozens of varieties of pastries and bread items, only to realize that her tummy was more than merely full from last night— it felt somewhat upset as well.

"I believe I'll have but a cappuccino with you, Alfredo," Millicent said. "I don't want to eat anything that might cause me to feel that old nasty nausea."

"I understand, darling. Why don't you find a table for us out on the terrace, and I'll bring out your cappuccino when ready."

That seemed like an excellent idea to Millicent. She turned and staggered out the front door and landed at a small table made of wrought iron, complete with four uncomfortable chairs shielded by an open, red-green-and-white umbrella with the word *Campari* written across the top.

Campari? she thought to herself as she sat. *Isn't that some kind of bitter Italian liqueur?*

The Case of the Magic Fluke

Unfortunately, merely thinking about alcohol at eight o'clock in the morning made her wretch and suddenly grow dizzy. Of course, being inside an overly warm bakery, the heavy air pungent with sweet and gooey smells, didn't help matters either. Slowly, Millicent bent over and placed her head between her knees.

After a few short minutes Millicent sat up, feeling somewhat better but still not one hundred per cent. Not by a long shot. At last Alfredo returned, boys in tow, carrying a bowl of water for the pugs and a plate full of pastries for both him and Millicent. One of the counter girls from inside the bakery placed the two double cappuccinos on the table, while Holmes and Watson, each with their mouths jammed with a sugar-encrusted, jelly-filled Austrian donut, slid under the table next to her feet.

"There we are, my darling," Alfredo said, placing the plate of goodies in front of her. Trying her best to ignore the sweets, Millicent said her thanks to both Alfredo and the serving girl before breathing in the healing properties of the aroma produced by the freshly pressed coffee.

"Those look lovely Alfredo," she said still without looking. "But I'm not sure I should indulge. My tummy still feels a bit queasy this morning, so I'll think I'll refrain from the sweets."

"Ah," he sighed, "I thought you might be feeling a bit under the weather. So I also picked out a bagel for you, as well as a pretzel, to perhaps fill you up, sì, but settle your stomach at the same time."

Even with a slightly queasy stomach, Millicent always had trouble saying no to fresh baked goods. "Mmmm, well," she stammered, "I may just have to try one of those tempting pretzels later."

She turned her gaze toward her feet. "And how about you boys? I see you have a sugary treat as well," she observed.

Holmes gave a short bark while Watson merely moaned.

"This morning I was hoping to have us visit a few of the lovely museums Salzburg has to offer, particularly Mozart's Geburtshaus," she said, staring at the lone pretzel on the plate.

"What's a gazoots-hoos?" Watson asked, his mouth still full.

"It's the house that one is brought home to from the hospital after being born," Holmes replied.

"Why yes," agreed Millicent, "or in Mozart's case, it's actually the home in which he was born."

For a very brief moment Watson stopped eating and thought deeply about that. "I not sure 'ow I feel about this. Will we see any more serpents or woodland creatures like last night?"

Millicent chuckled. "There's no need to worry, Watson," she said. "I can almost guarantee that nothing in the museum will cause you to stress over."

The small sips of the cappuccino were doing their job at making Millicent feel more like herself—so much more, in fact, that she decided to pick up the pretzel after all and give it a few nibbles. Pretzels generally made her feel not only better, but nearly ecstatic. And this morning was no exception. By the time the quartet got up to walk, Millicent was actually feeling much more chipper.

"Wha' er we going to do in a stuffy old museum, 'olmes?" Watson asked in a whisper.

Holmes cleared his throat. "We'll probably learn a few things," he answered, "which wouldn't hurt either one of us."

"I don't know why I 'ave to learn about somebody I don't even know," Watson continued.

"For your information, Mozart was a famous Austrian composer whose works are still played quite frequently today." Holmes was no expert in classical music, but he did know who Mozart was, particularly after the fiasco they'd all been through the night before.

The trot from the bakery to Mozart's Geburtshaus was not far, and with a good fifteen minutes before the doors of the museum would open, Millicent, Alfredo, Holmes, and Watson were able to take their time. As they strolled toward their destination, Holmes sniffed at everything he came across along the way, and Watson, of course, baptized with his piddle every plant, pebble, and protrusion.

"I certainly am grateful for that lovely massage yesterday," she remarked, when suddenly those odd feelings once again started to take over her body.

"Alfredo, I think I'm going to need to sit," she added through her teeth.

"What's the matter darling? Is it your back?" Alfredo's concern for Millicent took up every minute of the day and not merely because she was pregnant. Without being aware of it, Millicent could get herself into more trouble than bargained for. Luckily, however, Alfredo was usually at her side. And if not him, Holmes and Watson for sure.

"No," she said, "it's not my back. I suddenly feel quite drained. And I think my walnut-sized bladder is once again working hard to get my attention."

Holmes and Watson, hearing Millicent's dilemma, scampered ahead and found a small bench for her to sit. Immediately, they barked to draw her attention.

"Oh Alfredo," she said sprightly, "look what the boys found for me. As soon as the museum opens, I'll, of course, need to run to the ladies room. Yet from there on everything should be all right."

"If you are sure, *mia cara*," he said hesitantly. "It's no trouble for me to knock on the door and see if the docent has arrived. Perhaps whoever it is will open early given your situation."

Millicent wiggled from one buttock to another, doing her best to hold everything in that wanted to come out. "That might be a very good idea, Alfredo," she said. "I don't think I can wait much longer."

Alfredo always did as he was told, more or less, as long as it was

55

Millicent doing the telling. According to his watch in was nine o'clock, time for the museum to open. Yet when he walked up to the door, he realized it was still tightly locked. He looked back at Millicent to tell her as much, but saw from the strange look on her face that things were not going well for her.

He had no other recourse but to start pounding on the door—then yelling. Then pounding and yelling. When that didn't work, Holmes and Watson joined in as well with their barking, scratching at the door, and whining. At last a very old man—at least the oldest man Holmes and Watson had ever seen—opened the door slowly, looked at the trio suspiciously, but then smiled.

"*Es tut mir leit*. I'm terribly sorry," he said. "I was a bit late getting here this morning. In fact, I'd barely arrived when I heard you at the door. I'll be glad to usher you into the main rooms as soon as I turn on the lights and unlock the inner doors."

Without hesitation Holmes and Watson trotted in and upon Alfredo's command sat patiently on their haunches in what looked like a small hallway or foyer. Meanwhile, Alfredo ran back to Millicent, scooped her up, and walked with her as briskly as he could to the now-opened museum.

"Good morning, *buon giorno*," Alfredo said to the old man as soon as he and Millicent crossed the threshold. "I am Alfredo Martolini, and this is my wife, Millicent Winthrop Martolini. And you are?"

56

"*Guten Morgen*," the elderly docent replied. "I am Walter Winckelmann. It's my pleasure to meet you."

"Herr Winckelmann, if it's not too much trouble, would you mind hurrying sir?" Alfredo pressed. "My wife is eight months pregnant and desperate to use your ladies' room."

"A lady's room?" It was obvious to Millicent that Herr Winckelmann was a bit confused.

"*Die Damentoilette, bitte*," Millicent interrupted.

"Ah, ja. *Ich verstehe.* Please, give me a moment while I find the key."

The old man exited into a tiny room marked *Büro*, which Alfredo assumed was the office. "I'll just be a moment," the old gentleman called back to them. "I know I put it somewhere."

Standing rock still no longer worked for Millicent. And there really was no place to sit now that they were half way in the door, so the only thing she could do was pace. With Alfredo's arm wrapped around her, the two of them walked the length of the hallway, turned around to go back, only to turn around again and carefully make their way back up the hallway.

Holmes and Watson, desperate to help their mistress, could do nothing more than follow close behind.

Finally, Herr Winckelmann returned with a full set of keys in his hand. "Please, follow me. I know it must be one of these keys," he said as he trudged up the two flights of stairs leading to the museum proper. Holmes and Watson scampered close behind, while Alfredo practically carried Millicent, one stair at a time.

Once there the old man worked at unlocking the doors leading into the main rooms, one key at a time. It took several tries and several keys, but before he ran out of possibilities, the lock on the main door finally clicked. As soon as the double doors swung open, Millicent made a run for what was clearly marked as the restroom.

However, as she started to run across the floor, she noticed what looked like a man's pair of legs sticking out from under the lid of a small grand piano.

Oh my, she thought, *of course, that must have been Mozart's childhood piano. How grand is that?* She couldn't help but chuckle at her own pun.

"Excuse me," she said as she flew by to the protruding legs of whoever it was inside the piano, "I didn't realize you were tuning the composer's very piano."

When there was no immediate answer, she abruptly stopped, slowly turned in an about face, and gave Alfredo a look of pure horror. "I'm not seeing what I think I'm seeing, am I Alfredo?" she asked in a panic.

Alfredo looked in the direction where Millicent had nodded and quickly assessed the situation. He lifted the lid slowly and carefully, placed his fingers on the man's neck, and checked for a pulse.

Nothing. He tried again, but nothing.

"I'm afraid this man is dead," he said.

Without a moment's hesitation, Millicent screamed, then hiccupped three times in a row, ending with three exuberant high-pitched sneezes. Finally, she ended her string of vocal incantations with one long, deep-bellied burp. And as soon as she did, her bladder exploded.

***

It didn't take long for the police to arrive. Alfredo noticed right away how very kind they were regarding Millicent's situation and didn't hesitate for a minute to go back to their hotel to retrieve a change of clothes for her, which she quickly changed into after cleaning up. Also, word must've spread from their last FIFA case in Berlin, for once the authorities had heard who it was vacationing in their city, they immediately took notice.

"*Grüss Gott*," an official looking woman said to Millicent as soon as she returned from the WC back to Alfredo and the crime scene. "I'm Inspector Prachi Pesseingimpel, head detective assigned to this case. It's a pleasure to meet you in person, Frau Winthrop, er Martolini," she said, offering her hand. "I've heard so much about you and your husband. And I'm especially excited to be working together with you two on this case, should you agree to do so."

"How do you d—" Millicent began.

59

The Case of the Magic Fluke

"I'm afraid we're not able to assist you on this case, as we are on a much needed holiday here in Salzburg," Alfredo said, immediately interrupting Millicent. "And as you can see, my wife is very pregnant and shouldn't be put under any undue stress at this time."

"Oh, yes, I see that now," the inspector said chagrined. "It's just that having you both, along with your canine assistants, here in our fair city is more than a coincidence. In some ways, it's actually a most fortunate opportunity, not only for me in wrestling with this case, but for the general profession of crime solving as a whole. A real stroke of luck."

"Ah, a fluke, in other words," Millicent said, trying her best not to show her indecision regarding her possible intervention in the case. She was aware of Alfredo's concerns for her health and safety, as well as the need for the four of them to have the kind of recuperative holiday they'd earned and deserved. Not knowing what condition her former talents and powers of crime solving were in also made her vacillate. Yet something was tugging at her psyche, nudging her toward going against Alfredo's wishes and instead diving into the crime before her.

"Well, maybe as long as we're all here," she began again.

"Millicent, darling," Alfredo said, grabbing her by the elbow, "can I see you out in the hall for a moment?"

"Certainly," she answered smiling, all too aware that Alfredo may not on the same page as her. "Excuse us for a minute or so."

Holmes and Watson watched as the two lovebirds jetted out of the room.

***

"What's going on 'olmes?" Watson whispered.

"I suspect our mistress and master are not at this particular moment necessarily getting along."

"Yeah," Watson echoed, "getting along. So what should we do?"

"What we always do," Holmes said proudly, "investigate the premises, look for unusual happenstances and peculiarities, and then see what the evidence has to tell us."

"Right, 'appyglances and pickled rarities," Watson agreed, following his brother as they began their assignment.

Holmes stopped in his tracks. "No, Watson," he said after clearing his throat, "please do not follow me. You go left and I'll go to the right, and we'll meet somewhere in the middle to compare notes."

"Oh, yeah, compare notes."

"All right, now skedaddle," Holmes ordered, but again Watson trailed him close behind.

"Watson, what is your problem today?" Holmes was beginning to show his irritation at the little pug.

"You told me to go right and that you'd go to the left," he answered happily.

In frustration Holmes cleared his throat once again. "No I didn't."

"Ta, ya did," Watson said smugly. So smugly, in fact, that Holmes began to doubt himself.

"All right, then. You go ahead and go right then and allow me to be the one to go left," Holmes said as he crisscrossed in front of Watson.

In merely a matter of seconds, Holmes became aware that one again he was being followed by his littermate. "Bloody hell, Watson. Don't you know your left from your right?"

"Why, of course I do, 'olmes. See this is to my right," he said circling toward his right shoulder, "And this is to my left." Watson changed directions and circled toward his left.

The only problem, Holmes noticed, was he was turning a full circle before continuing on his way. "You're not turning right and left," he said impatiently. "You're merely turning clockwise and counterclockwise."

"Huh?"

"Never mind," Holmes said at last. "Just follow me then. We'll investigate this place as one."

"Yeah, as one," Watson said beaming. Well, beaming as much as a push-face pug could possibly beam.

Holmes then turned to his left, sure that Watson would follow. As soon as he did, however, he noticed Watson moving toward the right.

"I'll be waiting for you in the middle, Holmes," he said assuredly, and off he went.

"Oh, bugger," Holmes sighed to himself. "How Watson navigates through this world as well as he does, I'll never know."

***

Millicent had never seen Alfredo as angry as he seemed to be now. Not that she wasn't a bit peeved at him as well, but instead of saying her piece, she decided to remain quiet as he paced up and down the hallway floor.

"Millicent, you cannot take this assignment," he ranted, his flailing arms emphasizing his argument. "We need the rest. You need the rest. And don't forget your baby needs a rest."

"I know, Alfredo," she answered softly, trying her best to calm him down.

"The only reason I agreed to go on this holiday is because you promised it would be exactly that—a holiday."

"You're right, Alfredo," she agreed.

"I worry about you day and night. 'Should I rub her back? Should I walk the dogs? Should I put a tracking device in her tote so if she gets lost again I can find her?' Taking care of you is a twenty-four hour job."

Millicent stood silent for nearly a full minute. She felt quite stung by Alfredo's words, yet she knew they were true. She was a handful, and she was grateful day and night for Alfredo's loving attention and care.

The Case of the Magic Fluke

"Actually, I think you should always rub my back," she answered, "and my feet, too. And I know Holmes and Watson love it when you take them on long walks. It not only gives them a chance to do their business, but helps to provide for them a sense of adventure."

"Ah, my darling," Alfredo said as he took her in his arms.

"And, as far as the tracking device goes, I think that would be absolutely brilliant. Then no matter what happens, I'll always know that you'll somehow find and rescue me."

"*Mia cara,* I love you so much, Millicent" he said, rubbing her lower back. "It's only that I want the very best for you and the baby."

"Oooooo, keep that up, please," she said dreamily, her eyes closed. "I want that for you too, Alfredo. But we cannot choose when our help is needed in solving a crime, for helping others is so much more than what we do. It's who we are."

"Ah, sweetheart you always know how to get me to change my mind," he said. "All right, we can help the police, but you must promise me you'll be careful and not over extend yourself. Sì?"

"Of course, my love," Millicent said, staring up into Alfredo's dreamy brown eyes. Then crossing her fingers she added, "I'll be good, I promise."

Alfredo bent down as best he could given Millicent's very large baby bump and gently kissed his clever wife, knowing full well that once again she'd worked her magic, causing him to give in.

Chapter 5

Holmes and Watson set about their separate tasks of sniffing out the joint—both literally and figuratively. Inspector Pesseingimpel curiously noted the two of them from time to time, but was intermittingly distracted by the arrival of the forensics crew, followed by the coroner. It wasn't until she saw each of the canine assistants scampering full speed toward one another, barking on the top of their tiny lungs, that she stopped what she was doing and ordered them to halt.

"I've got it," Watson sputtered.

"No, I've got it," Holmes retorted.

"You're too slow, 'olmes, always 'ave been. I tell ya, I've got it."

"I'll show you slow!" As soon as Holmes said that, he slammed on his brakes, and slid headfirst into Watson. Both dogs immediately chomped down onto what looked like a something small, out of place, and important.

Because neither one of them wanting to let go, together they trotted proudly up to the inspector and dropped what was in their mouth directly in front of her feet.

"What's this you've found?" she asked curiously. Holmes and Watson looked at each other in confusion. It never ceased to make them curious as to why people would ask them a question, when they knew full well there'd be no way they'd be able to understand their answer.

As soon as the inspector picked it up, she realized it was a wallet. She picked it up carefully, as it was now covered in pug saliva, and took it over to the forensics team to clean up.

"Good dogs," the inspector said. "I suspect we would've found this eventually, but your help and expediting this case is greatly appreciated."

Holmes and Watson immediately sat on their haunches. "Do you think she's going to give us a treat?" Watson asked Holmes, who was still catching his breath.

"I doubt it," he said between huffs. "She obviously is not a dog owner or she would already have given us what we both deserve."

Inspector Pesseingimpel had just been given the wallet back and was carefully placing all of its contents—paper receipts, money credit cards—on the Mozart family dining table when Alfredo and Millicent walked into the room. The last thing she fished out was the driver's license belonging to who she suspected was their victim.

"Oh my God," she said, staring at the photo in front of her. "I know this person."

"You do?" Alfredo and Millicent asked simultaneously.

"Yes, I believe I do. If I'm not mistaken he's the local girls' football coach here in Salzburg. His name is Felix Fuchs. And he has quite a history with the police in this town."

Millicent took the license from her and showed it to Alfredo. "Really? And how's that?"

"Mostly complaints regarding his treatment of his players and staff. Look," the inspector said, taking back the license, "once the coroner finishes with his examination, we will check his face against his identification."

"And when do you think that will be?" Alfredo asked.

Inspector Prachi Pesseingimpel was all too familiar with the reputation of Salzburg's coroner, Doctor Linus Lustgarten. She knew him to be extremely thorough, which meant he most likely wouldn't be finished until early afternoon.

"I suspect it will be a little while. In the meantime why don't you two make yourselves comfortable on that settee?" she said pointing to a small brocaded bench against the wall.

"I'm afraid the police and I will be using the dining room table and chairs as we sort out this mess."

***

Alfredo was about to take Millicent's arm and escort her to the small uncomfortable looking settee, when she instead took him by his elbow and led him out of the building.

"Come, Holmes," she said, "you too, Watson."

"Where are we going Millicent?" Alfredo asked.

"I think we need to take a little walk around this building. Something about this murder just doesn't feel right," she said as they descended the stairs. By the time they reached street level, she'd hiccupped her signature three times in a row.

"What do you mean, darling?" Alfredo was on the alert, for whenever Millicent let out a string of hiccups or sneezes, it usually meant something important about whatever case they were working on was about to be said or discovered.

"Well, first of all, I felt sick all morning, yet as soon as I saw the dead body, I felt one hundred percent better. And it wasn't just because I'd finally tinkled." This time her words were followed by four or five high-pitched sneezes.

"You think your illness then is tied to this murder?" Alfredo asked expectantly.

"I'm not sure," she said, "but it wouldn't surprise me if it indeed was."

"And so why are we outside again?" Alfredo asked.

Millicent took Alfredo by the hand and motioned for Holmes and Watson to join them as they circled their way toward the back of the building.

"You and I both saw the head wound, right?" she continued. "Like you I at first assumed that it was the killing blow. But then I had to ask myself, 'why is there no blood on, near, or underneath Mozart's piano?' And the only explanation that made any sense to me is that the dead man was not a piano tuner."

"We both know that, Millicent," Alfredo said, trying his best not to chuckle.

"Sorry, I couldn't help myself. But seriously, I'm convinced that the gentleman must've been killed elsewhere and his body then placed in the museum for who knows what reason."

"Ah, I see what you're getting at," Alfredo agreed. "So . . . tell me again what it is we're doing out here?"

"It's obvious to me that whoever staged that man's body at the piano definitely did not come through the front door."

"You don't think Herr Winckelmann had anything to do with it, do you?"

Once again Millicent started to giggle. "No, I don't think he had anything to do with it. He's a bit on the weak side, far too old, and not quite all there upstairs, if you know what I mean."

"Sì, this is true."

"So be on the lookout, Alfredo, for anything that might look out of place. And that goes for you boys, too."

Relying on Alfredo's steady arm, Millicent leaned over to speak directly to her two canine assistants. "You've already got the victim's scent from the wallet you retrieved. See if can now uncover how the killer was able to stash the man's body inside this second floor museum. Have you got that?" she asked.

Both Holmes and Watson nodded their heads and gave a short yip. Soon they were off once again sniffing their way through the streets of Salzburg.

***

While the boys took off, Alfredo and Millicent carefully strolled down the avenue of small shops, hoping to find a way to the back of the building. What they soon discovered was there wasn't one.

"Bugger," Millicent said angrily, "I was sure there was a back to the building, for I distinctly remember seeing a courtyard out one of the windows near the women's restroom. Of course, whether or not it led to a back entrance of the museum is yet to be seen."

"Perhaps the only way to a back courtyard is through the downstairs entryway, down the hallway and beyond the office, and then out a back door or window," Alfredo said.

"I don't remember seeing one, did you?" she asked, still frustrated.

"No, but that doesn't mean it's not there," he said, doing his best to calm her down. "First, however, we'd better go find Holmes and Watson before they get lost."

"You mean before we get lost," Millicent said with a chuckle. "Yes, let's go back. Besides, Inspector Pesseingimpel must be wondering where we've gone to."

"True," he agreed, "and perhaps by now the coroner is finished with his examination and can give us more information."

"You're right Alfredo," she said. "It will help us all the more in solving this case once the victim has been identified."

As the two slowly made their way back to the scene of the crime, they intermittently called out for Holmes and Watson, but to no avail.

"I wonder what could have happened to them," Alfredo said.

"Yes, it's not like them to wander far," Millicent answered. "In fact, the only time I remember Watson running off was when in Venice he chased after a tray of fresh sausages, which he then made off with. It took everything I had to stop him from getting arrested."

"Or be ground up into a sausage himself," Alfredo added jokingly. "We Venetians take great pride of ownership in our freshly made sausages."

"That gives me an idea," Millicent said. "Follow me."

The Case of the Magic Fluke

The Martolinis took their time strolling back to the museum by weaving in and out of all the little shops and bistros on their way. They had nearly reached their destination when Millicent spotted a small wrought iron sign hanging outside the door of a small delicatessen.

It read *Käsekrainer* with a painted picture in full color of two interesting looking sausages painted on its center.

"I'll bet you anything they're in there," Millicent said. "And to tell you the truth, I'm starting to become somewhat hungry myself. Are you?"

"I didn't think I was," Alfredo added, "but those sausages on the sign look too good to pass up."

As soon as Alfredo opened the door, he and Millicent saw the two missing pugs sitting at a small café table, feasting on a small plate of cut up sausages.

"Fancy meeting you here," Alfredo said to Holmes and Watson, who both turned with a start.

"We've been looking for you everywhere," Millicent added. "And where did these sausages come from?"

Her two canine assistants nearly choked.

"That man over dere be'ind the counter gave 'em to us," Watson said, his mouth so stuffed full of sausages that pieces of it were tumbling out and rolling across the table as he spoke.

"Did he give them to you or did you take them?" Alfredo asked, doing his best to sound stern when what he really wanted to do was laugh.

Holmes cleared his throat. "Actually, when the man saw us sitting in front of his deli case, he was so surprised to see us, and without a master or mistress in sight, that he dropped his freshly made sausages onto the floor. Watson then went for them, but the man snatched them up before Watson could steal them. We were about to leave, when he suddenly offered them to us, all cut up nicely and sitting on this lovely plate. We been munching on them ever since."

"Is that true?" Millicent asked the man behind the counter.

"Is what true, meine Frau?"

"Did you give Holmes and Watson some of your sausages or did they steal them?" Alfredo asked.

The man started to laugh. "*Nein*, they did not steal them, but I'm sure the little black one would have had I not scooped them up off the floor in time to give them a quick wash before serving."

"And they 'ave bits of cheese in 'em too," Watson added.

Millicent took a moment to think Watson's words through. Finally, she asked, "And what kind of cheese do you put in your sausages?"

"Why, only the very best Emmentaler from our Swiss neighbors, of course. Then I hickory smoke them until they are perfection," he said. "May I interest you and your man in a small plate? I'll even add a side of my own freshly brined sauerkraut—no charge."

The Case of the Magic Fluke

As if on cue, Millicent's stomach growled as she looked longingly toward Alfredo. "Does that sound good to you, Alfredo?"

Alfredo was not a keen sausage eater, but any chance to accept a bargain, even if it was only a side of sauerkraut, was okay in his book. "That sounds splendid," he said as he returned Millicent's smile.

"Brilliant," she said, turning back to the man, "and let's make that two small plates, *bitte*."

***

As soon as the quartet returned to the composer's birth house, they checked out the rear access to the courtyard behind the building from off the ground floor. It was nothing to speak of—merely an old door boarded up and heavily locked.

Disappointed but not dissuaded, Millicent decided to try one more time by asking Herr Winckelmann if she might take a look out the small window in the historic kitchen area of the home.

"There's something else we need to look at, Alfredo, before I toss out my initial idea."

"Certainly darling," he said. "Let me help you up the stairs."

"Please, let's make our way up slowly, examining the steps themselves as well as the railing to see if anything looks askew."

"What's *ask you* mean 'olmes?" Watson asked.

"Not 'ask you,' you dunder head," Holmes blurted. "*Askew*, as in something is not quite right."

"Like the performance at the puppet theater last night," Watson said. "Those marionettes were totally *askew*."

Holmes wanted to say, *yes, especially after you mangled and tangled them up*, but instead he merely rolled his eyes and ascended the staircase, sniffing each riser and spindle as he made his way. Watson followed close behind.

By the time everyone made it up to the Mozart apartment, Millicent was nearly dizzy with concern. "I don't understand how I could be so far off base," she said to the other three, but mostly to herself. "Perhaps he *was* murdered in this room after all, and then the killer merely cleaned the floor and furniture after the event."

"If that's true, darling," Alfredo said, "then I'm sure a luminol test on the piano, the floor underneath it, and these steps would give us the answer we're looking for."

"Yes, of course," she said, slightly distracted.

Inspector Pesseingimpel was waiting for them as they walked into the main museum room. "The coroner has finished his examination," she said," and I was right. The victim is indeed Felix Fuchs. He's been taken to the police assigned mortuary where his wife Friedl Fuchs will soon arrive to make a full personal identification."

"You mentioned earlier that he already had a record on file with the police," Alfredo said.

"Yes that's correct," she said. "It was filed by a Silke Schlumpf a few months ago. Apparently Felix had made some derogatory remarks about her size and sexual orientation, which the young woman took offense."

"And is she your number one suspect thus far?" Millicent asked.

"Yes, her and, of course, the docent, Walter Winckelmann. Because of his age I was ready to dismiss him as a possible suspect until I heard his story. Apparently Herr Winckelmann had an altercation with Felix during one of his granddaughter's soccer games. According to him, Herr Fuchs was not a very kind or gracious man."

"But Herr Winckelmann seems to be a very kind and gracious man himself," Alfredo said. "It's difficult to imagine him capable of such a thing."

"I agree," the inspector continued, "but he was the only person here in the building before the victim was discovered by the four of you. Perhaps if he didn't commit the murder himself, he may have been an accessory. Who else could have opened the door and let the killer and victim into the museum proper?"

"Well, whoever it was," Millicent said, "they either murdered him in this room or killed him elsewhere, then brought him here to the museum, raised the lid of Mozart's grand piano, lifted up the body, and shoved him in among the piano strings."

"Ja, you're right," the inspector said. "I hadn't thought of it that way."

"What would help us immensely inspector," Alfredo said, "would be if you could luminol the room as well as the stairs leading up to this floor."

"I can do that," she said as she jotted the information down in her small detective's notebook.

"Then if you would give us a list of all those who may have either formally registered a complaint against Herr Fuchs or were rumored to have said disparaging remarks about the man, then Alfredo and I will interview them and pass whatever we learn over to you."

"I'll make sure the forensics team also sweeps for fingerprints," the inspector said.

"That's fine, Inspector" said Millicent, "but I doubt you'll find anything conclusive. The murderer has thought this crime out in detail, which is why I doubt they'd be foolish enough to leave their fingerprints behind."

"I suppose you're right, but it doesn't hurt to try," she said. "I'll get that list over to you immediately. Is there anything else I should do before we talk again?"

"No, I don't think so. Alfredo and I are now on our way to the mortuary to introduce ourselves to Frau Fuchs and ask her a few questions," Millicent said. "Before Alfredo and I go any further into this investigation, we definitely want to hear what she has to say about this murder and about the complaints against her husband."

"That sounds good. I'll be sure to keep you up to date with any news I hear from the forensics crew or the coroner. And I'm sure you'll do the same for me."

"Of course, we most certainly will," Alfredo said.

"Yes," Millicent agreed. "We will be in touch."

***

Even though the distance between the Geburtshaus and the University of Salzburg where the autopsy was being held was walkable, Millicent was beginning to fade. Her lower back was killing her, and once again her ankles had swollen in the summer heat. It was decided instead to take a taxi, since taking Holmes and Watson was somewhat frowned down upon by the city bus drivers. No sooner had they all stuffed themselves into the small Mercedes taxi than Alfredo's cell phone buzzed.

"Pronto."

"Alfredo, Mr. Smythe here. How are you and Millicent enjoying your holiday? Does the hotel please you?"

"Millicent and I and the boys are doing fine. And the hotel you provided for us is *molto bellisima.*"

"Is that Mr. Smythe on your mobile" Millicent asked excitedly. "Oooh, I want to speak with him when you're finished."

As soon as Holmes and Watson realized who was on the phone, they yipped happily, causing their front legs to leave the comforting laps of both Alfredo and Millicent.

Alfredo quickly handed his phone to Millicent. "Tell him about the murder, darling," he mouthed silently so Mr. Smythe wouldn't hear.

"Hallo Bucky," she said, "Helmut sends his regards. And so do Holmes and Watson. We've already been to the hotel's restaurant, which was out of this world, and we attended a performance of Mozart's *The Magic Flute* at the marionette theatre last night."

"And how did the four of you enjoy that?" Mr. Smythe inquired.

"Well, let's just say it was a memorable evening."

"I take it Watson was up to his usual high jinks, yes?"

"Ah, you know us so well," she said with a giggle. "So what brings this phone call?"

"I hate to be the harbinger of bad tidings, but I'm afraid FIFA's been notified of a potential murder of one of our coaches."

"It wouldn't happen to be the Felix Fuchs case, would it?" she asked. "Alfredo and I were at the crime scene this morning and have been doing a bit of investigation to assist the police here in Salzburg."

Mr. Smythe sighed. "I'm so sorry to ask this of you and Alfredo, but we need a presence on this case, and I have no one else to cover it but you two—with the help of Holmes and Watson, of course."

"I understand, Bucky, but I think you'd better run this past Alfredo. He's voiced to me his reservations, but he should share them with you as well." Millicent handed the phone back to Alfredo and proceeded to do her best to calm the dogs down.

"What's this I hear, Alfredo? Tell me what's on your mind." Mr. Smythe and Alfredo had a good relationship, which Mr. Smythe wanted to retain.

"It's just that Millicent is so tired, her back hurts, her ankles are swollen, and any day now she may deliver *il nostro piccolo bambino*. I don't think it's wise for us to involve ourselves in this new case, but I will defer to you to make the decision."

"I understand Alfredo, and if I had anyone else who could cover this case, I wouldn't have called on you. Tell you what, should working on solving this crime get to be too much, call me and I'll take over. In the meantime, take it easy, try to keep Millicent from going into one of her trances, and put more responsibility onto the boys. They know what to do by now."

Alfredo took a minute to think over Mr. Smythe's words. He also remembered what Millicent had said about helping others find justice for their loved ones and agreed. Even though it was not his first choice, he decided to go along with Mr. Smythe's suggestion.

"You can count on all four of us, Mr. Smythe," he said. "But don't be surprised if you hear from me before this crime is solved."

Chapter 6

Alfredo was about ready to call for a taxi when Millicent suggested that they travel by a Fiaker instead.

"Wassa faker, 'olmes," the always curious Watson asked.

"Not a faker, but a Fiaker. It's one of those horse drawn carts you see everywhere here in Salzburg," Millicent answered.

"What's that darling," Alfredo asked, unsure if he heard her right.

"I'd like us to take one of those open air, horse drawn coaches to the hospital instead of an old boring taxi," Millicent said.

Alfredo thought about that for a moment. "As long as you think the boys will not overreact to the horses and try to jump out of the cart, then I'm all for it," he declared.

"I'll make sure Watson and I stay within the bounds of

the carriage, madam," Holmes said reassuringly.

"Thank you Holmes. I know I can always count on you," she said.

It took some time for the Fiaker to arrive, but once everybody was in and secured in their seats, off they went. As they rode through the Alstadt, the old section of the city, they could not help but be stunned by the exquisite beauty of the city gardens and Baroque architecture.

"I'm so very pleased you suggested this Millicent," Alfredo said. "I can't think of a better way to take in this gorgeously sunny weather. At last I feel as if I'm truly on holiday. Don't you agree, darling?"

No answer.

"Millicent, I asked you if you agree," Alfredo pressed. Looking over at his glowing wife, he noticed her chin resting on her chest, but instead of hearing her answer, Millicent produced the lovely purr of a snore.

"Driver," he said softly, "for the next half hour or so would you please drive us around to all the sites of the city? My wife desperately needs this nap, and so I hesitate to wake her."

"With pleasure, signore," the driver answered in his thick Austrian accent.

At that moment Alfredo felt Millicent's body slide toward him and rest against his side. He gently put his arm around her and laid her head proudly on his chest.

"Sleep well, my darling," he said. "I have a feeling this case is going to require all of our combined strength to solve."

It didn't take long for Holmes and Watson to follow suit. The collective snores from

Alfredo's three fellow travelers caused his heart to swell. Soon his family would be increased by his and Millicent's new baby, and he couldn't imagine how his life could be any better than it was at this moment. Nonetheless he closed his eyes and allowed the gentle clip-clop of the horses to also lull him into slumber.

***

Alfredo wasn't exactly sure how much time had gone by before he heard his cell phone ring. In order to get to his mobile, he first had to prop Millicent up, thereby causing her eyes to gently open.

"Pronto," he said as soon as he answered the phone.

"Herr Martolini," Inspector Pesseingimpel greeted, "I wanted to let you know that Frau Fuchs has indeed identified the body as that of her husband and is in the hospital chapel now waiting for your arrival."

"Thank you, inspector," Alfredo answered, trying his best to not sound as if he'd just woken up. "We're on our way now and should be there any minute."

Holmes always slept with his eyes open, so to let Alfredo know he was awake, he merely lifted his head and snorted. Watson was still out cold.

"How long have I been asleep?" Millicent asked with a yawn.

The Case of the Magic Fluke

Alfredo glanced at his wristwatch. "I'm only guessing, but I'd say at least an hour."

"An hour," Millicent blurted, "how could I have been asleep of a whole hour?"

"We've all been napping, *mia cara*. I think our travels have started to catch up with us."

Watson at last lifted his head, and with his eyes still closed said, "Yeah, catch up with us." The then sneezed twice and turned over.

The coach slowed in front of the local hospital—then stopped.

"That was the inspector on the phone. Frau Fuchs is waiting for us in the hospital chapel," Alfredo said.

"And has she identified the body?"

"Yes," he answered," she has. The victim is indeed her husband Felix Fuchs."

"Well, I'm not sorry I slept," Millicent admitted, "for now I feel so much better than I did earlier."

Alfredo smiled lovingly at his wife. "I'm delighted to hear that, my darling. Let me pay our driver what we owe, and then the four of us will see what information we can garner from Frau Fuchs."

***

When they arrived at the chapel, it didn't take a genius to figure out who the woman seated in one of the wooden pews was, for not only

84

was Frau Fuchs the only visitor present, she was crying her eyes out.

"Oh, my God," she wailed, "my dear sweet Felix is gone."

Millicent tiptoed toward her and stood, leaving Alfredo and the dogs behind. "Frau Fuchs," she said softly, "I'm Millicent Winthrop, and I'm here with my husband, Alfredo Martolini, and our two canine assistants, Holmes and Watson. We first want to tell you that we are so very sorry for your loss. I can't imagine losing someone you love and to whom you've been married for as many years as you have."

The woman wiped her eyes and blew her nose before looking up at Millicent . "Please," she said, "call me Friedl."

"By all means, Frau Fuchs . . . er . . . Friedl. Frau Friedl Fuchs." Millicent wasn't sure why, but for some reason simply saying that woman's name nearly forced a giggle. *Don't laugh,* she told herself, *whatever you do, please do not laugh.*

Quickly Millicent cleared her throat. "My husband and I are private investigators working for Mr. Smythe, head of the Security Council at FIFA headquarters. I understand your husband was a women's football coach?"

"Yes," answered the Frau, "soccer was his life. The team was his life. We never had any children, so the girls on the team were to him like his own."

"And do you know of any reason why someone would want him dead?" Alfredo asked as he and the dogs sauntered up.

Frau Fuchs scooted into the row to allow Millicent to sit on her left. Alfredo along with Holmes and Watson entered the same pew but from the opposite end. Soon he, Holmes, and Watson were sitting to her right.

"No, I don't," the woman sobbed, before blowing her nose for a second time.

"We understand that in the past he had a disagreement with one of his players—a Silke Schlumpf," Millicent said. "Could you help explain their relationship to us?"

"That woman is one of the most annoying creatures on this planet," the Frau bit out. "She made Felix's life a living hell. And mine too, for that matter."

"Do you have any idea what set her off?" Alfredo asked.

"I really have no idea," she answered. "All I know is that she's a major complainer, and most of the people who set her off are men. Honestly, I think she has some kind of a man-hate issue."

"What you mean by that?" Millicent asked.

"It's just that her complaints are always about how men take advantage of her, don't give her a chance to help out with the team in terms of coaching, or disrespect her by saying things about her size, her looks, and the obvious scowl permanently etched on her face."

"Do you think she's capable of murder?" Alfredo asked as he jotted in his notebook.

"I think all of us are capable of murder at some point in our lives," she answered. "All I know is she hated my husband with a passion, and she made no secret of it."

"You wouldn't happen to know where we could find her, do you Friedl?" Millicent asked.

"I suspect she's still at work," Friedl answered tersely. "She owns and manages some ridiculous gym. And from what I can tell, she caters mostly to women bodybuilders. You know the type I mean."

Millicent really didn't know what type of woman would be interested in bodybuilding as she had never once in her life entered the doors of a gym. Her idea of bodywork was a healthy massage from Helmut. Or a luxurious bubble bath. Or even a double serving of Venice's own famous tiramisu-inspired gelato. But no, never had she ever entertained the art of weightlifting.

"And do you know where this gym is located?" Alfredo continued.

"I'm not sure," she said. "Somewhere near the Mirabelle Gardens, I believe."

Millicent took the woman's hands and in her own. "Friedl, if you need someone to talk to or have a question about the investigation, don't hesitate to call or get a hold of us. We're staying at the Luxury Hotel located on the Salzach."

Alfredo handed her a card with both his and Millicent's contact information on it, which she immediately placed in her purse.

"*Danke sehr*, thank you so much," she said. "I may at some point need to take advantage of your offer, but for right now I just want to sit here and cry."

And she did.

In fact it was sometime before she even came up for air.

"I think we'd better go, Alfredo," Millicent said in a whisper as she tiptoed away.

"Sì, of course." Alfredo led Holmes and Watson out of the chapel as quietly as he could. Once outside of the hospital Millicent placed her hand into Alfredo's. "That poor woman," she said. "If the stories of his philandering are true, how she must've suffered through all the years of that marriage."

"Do you think she suffered enough to kill her husband?" Alfredo asked.

"I'm not sure," Millicent said, "but I don't doubt for a minute that her sorrow is real."

"I agree," Alfredo said. "Let me call a taxi for us. Do you feel well enough to stop by Schlumpf's fitness studio on our way back to the hotel?"

"I think we should," she agreed. "Fräulein Schlumpf is the best lead we've had so far."

As Alfredo was about to make his call, Prachi Pesseingimpel pulled up in front of the hospital in one of Salzburg's famous blue, white, and orange police cars—siren a-blaring and lights a-twirling. To make matters worse, as soon as she stopped, the inspector laid on her horn—signaling for Holmes to start his barking and Watson his howling.

"So much for maintaining quiet in a hospital zone," Alfredo said.

"Oh, don't be so hard on her," Millicent scolded. "She's merely trying to get our attention."

Millicent and her entourage made their way to the idling police car. When within shouting range, the inspector rolled down her window. "Can I offer you a ride to wherever it is you are headed?"

"How very nice of you to ask," Millicent said, sliding into the front seat while Holmes and Watson joined Alfredo in the back.

"Perhaps if you would turn off your siren, then the dogs will settle down," Alfredo said through clenched teeth.

Immediately, the inspector switched off the siren. "I'm so sorry," she said. "I'm so used to it that I don't even hear it anymore. So, where can I take you?"

"I think it's best we pay a visit to Ms. Silke Schlumpf and see what she has to say about our murder," Millicent suggested.

"I have her address if you need it," the inspector offered.

"Frau Fuchs suggested we visit her at her place of work," Alfredo chimed in. "And she already gave us the address."

The Case of the Magic Fluke

This wasn't exactly true, but Alfredo wanted Millicent to be able to move freely in her investigation without being overseen by the police every time she made a move. He also knew that his wife was aware that he didn't exactly lie, but he did stretch the truth a bit. In other words, he and Millicent knew the Schlumpf woman worked at a gym. But had they been given an address? No.

"That's super," Inspector Pesseingimpel said, obviously not put off by Alfredo's clipped remarks. "Give it to me, and I'll take you there at once."

Suddenly it grew very quiet as the Martolini's realized how clever the inspector truly was. Finally, it was Millicent who spoke up.

"On second thought," she said, "I think it best we return to our hotel for tea and a short rest. My stomach ache is returning, and I also must use the restroom again. I swear I piddle more than both Holmes and Watson combined."

She then laughed, hoping that her humor would lighten the moment and ease any tension that may be forming between the inspector, Alfredo, and her. Fortunately, Prachi smiled and chortled at Millicent's situation.

"How well I know," she said. "I have three children of my own. And even though the little one is already four years old, I still have to plan my day around where I can stop to utilize the nicest and easiest to get to *Toiletten* in town."

"See, Alfredo," Millicent said with a giggle. "I'm not the only one."

Alfredo merely stared out the window.

***

Due to Prachi's expert, no-nonsense driving, the four arrived at the hotel within minutes—which was a good thing since after that ride, Millicent desperately needed the W.C. They said their good-byes to the inspector, promising to keep her in the loop as they questioned the suspects one by one, which so far there *was* only one. Millicent, unable to wait for the slow elevator, ran up the stairs to their suite in just a nick of time—all this while Alfredo took Holmes and Watson out for a short walk in order to do their business.

He didn't know why he was feeling so angry, but there was no denying it. And he hated himself for feeling that way. *Am I angry at Millicent?* he asked himself. *No, not with my darling Millicent.*

He and the boys walked a little further while he stewed. *Perhaps I'm only mad at myself,* he pondered. *Maybe*—indeed, for he'd been angry with himself many a time in the past, but this odd lump in his gut felt somehow different.

Ah, he sighed, *I'm probably only upset that this holiday has turned into another work week for all of us and not the relaxing holiday I'd hoped for and imagined.*

"But no one is at fault, are they *i miei piccolo carlini*?" he asked Holmes and Watson. Immediately, the two barked as if they understood what he had asked. "I'll take that as an affirmative," Alfredo added as they walked back toward the hotel to meet up with Millicent.

He knew something was still bothering him, and although he was a little closer to figuring it out, try as he may he couldn't put his finger on it.

***

Feeling much relieved and a bit energized, Millicent flew out the doors of the hotel and waddled as quickly as she could toward where Alfredo and the boys stood.

"Shall we get a move on?" she asked brightly, catching up with them.

"Si, we shall," Alfredo answered lovingly. "I looked up the address of Schlumpf's gym on my mobile. It's near the Mirabel Gardens, which should be an easy walk for us."

"Brilliant," Millicent answered. "And when we're finished with this interview, let's see if we can find some fun place for dinner—perhaps at an Italian trattoria? I'm feeling the urge for a plateful of pasta."

Holmes and Watson once again barked in approval. Millicent bent down to scratch the two of them behind their ears. "You'd enjoy that, wouldn't you?" she asked them.

Instantly, Holmes and Watson took off, pulling Alfredo at the end of their leash, and with Millicent speed walking to catch up.

"No matter how tired Holmes and Watson are, as soon as they think food is in the itinerary, they're ready to go again," Alfredo observed.

Millicent chuckled. "They're not the only ones. I'm always up for a good meal."

"Or a snack," Holmes offered.

"Or an amaretto biscotti," Watson added.

"Or a pretzel or two," Alfredo said with a smile. "Sì, dinner at an Italian Ristorante is definitely on our agenda this evening."

***

Millicent placed her arm through Alfredo's as they took their time sauntering toward the gym. They were quiet, but that didn't mean the gears in Millicent's head weren't churning a mile a minute.

I wonder what's going on with Alfredo? she asked herself. He seems so quiet—grumpy almost. That's certainly not like him. I know he's not angry or upset at me—that's obvious from the way he treats me with utmost kindness and gentility. But he's obviously in a mood, and I don't know what to do about it.

No sooner had they gone a few more meters, than Millicent could no longer stand being quiet. She decided to take the tactic with Alfredo that had worked so well before in the past—feigned bewilderment, which would hopefully allow Alfredo to speak honestly to her and without secrets.

"Alfredo," she asked gingerly, "is something the matter? You seem to be in an unusual mood—clearly not yourself."

"No. Why do you ask?"

The Case of the Magic Fluke

"I couldn't help but notice that you've been silent for most of the afternoon, and I wondered if there was anything on your mind that you'd like to share with me."

There was a moment of silence before Alfredo answered. "I really don't know what kind of mood I'm in, but I suspect it has something to do with this case."

"I know what you mean," she said. "I think it's thrown us all for a loop. I know I'm disappointed that we can't just spend the holiday together without having to work, but unfortunately that's not a choice we can make. Mr. Smythe is counting on us, the Salzburg police are counting on us, and I believe Friedl Fuchs is as well."

"I know, my darling," he answered, "and when you put it that way, I know I need to snap out of it, as you say. But for some reason I just can't."

Again Alfredo grew quiet.

"It's just that I don't want to spoil the time we have together whether we're working on this case or any other, for that matter," Millicent continued. "We should be happy, whether at work or at play. After all, we're happily married, we're soon to have this lovely little baby in our lives, and we're in a place in our careers where others actually respect us and expect us to do our best."

"I know Millicent," Alfredo agreed, "and it's true. I do enjoy being with you and Holmes and Watson. And I honestly don't think I have an issue with working on the case itself. It's just that normally we work together as a twosome, and then report what we've discovered to Mr. Smythe, and not to the local police."

"You're referring to Inspector Prachi Pesseingimpel?"

"I suppose I am," he admitted. "Whenever she comes around, she deflects to you. It's as if I'm invisible. I may as well not be present at all."

"Rubbish Alfredo," Millicent said, squeezing his arm, "I depend upon you one hundred per cent of the time. We've never met the inspector before, but based thus far on her reliance on us, she's either new at the job or doesn't know exactly what she should be doing next—which is why we must help her all we can. Yes?"

"All I'm saying darling," Alfredo continued, "is that I feel like the odd man out. You know the phrase *due è compagnia, ma tre è una* folla—two's company and three's a crowd? I believe that's how I feel right now. She's pulling you away from me at a time I believe we need each other the most."

Millicent silently allowed Alfredo's words to sink in and soon realized he was right. They were slowly drifting apart. Something had to be done and fast.

"I have an idea," Millicent said finally, "why don't we speak to Mr. Smythe this evening about this situation. I'm sure he'll be able to advise and help us to get things back on track."

Alfredo stopped and took Millicent by the shoulders. "Of course, *mia cara,"* he said, "I knew you'd be able to come up with a good solution."

He then pulled her toward him and kissed her, which isn't the easiest thing to do with a sizable baby bump wedged in between. So in the stillness of the next few moments he simply held her, stroked her beautiful hair, and whispered sweet words of his native Italian into her tiny ear. Millicent knew he was doing his best to reassure her that all was well again between the two of them, but she still wasn't fully convinced. Yet for now she decided not to share her qualms but rather keep her eye on the situation over the next few days.

Chapter 7

The building that housed Women's Total Fitness—the gym owned and operated by Silke Schlumpf—was a two-story affair with stairs—no lift, to Millicent's regret—leading up to a large open room wrapped in floor-to-ceiling windows. Even before Millicent and the troop charged toward the steps, through those windows she viewed several women working out on various apparatuses, including treadmills, elliptical machines, stationary bikes, and free weights. She concentrated hard to imagine which one of those women might indeed be the suspect, but try as she may, nothing came up.

When they finally arrived on the top floor, they entered the studio, where a young girl seated at the counter greeted them.

"May I help you?" she asked, chewing a large wad of gum at the same time.

"Yes, I hope you can," Millicent answered, somewhat out of breath. "I'm Millicent Winthrop, and this is my husband, Alfredo Martolini. We were wondering if we might have a word with your manager, Frau Silke Schlumpf. We understand she's the owner of this establishment, correct?"

"Yep, that's her," the girl said. "Silke's probably in her office now, so I'll go on back and let her know you're here. Can I tell her what this is concerning?"

Alfredo and the dogs stepped forward. "Please tell her it has to do with Felix Fuchs."

"Herr Fuchs, really?" the girl said chopping away. "That guy's a first-rate nutcase, if he asked me."

Millicent perked up her ears. "What makes you say that?"

The girl rolled her eyes. "Just that he comes in here at least once a week ranting and raving about which one of his players is doing this or which one of the referees at one of his recent games is doing that. He complains all the time about everything. But Silke is the one he constantly dumps on the most."

"Do the two of them ever get into it with each other?" Alfredo asked, pulling out his small notebook to once again jot things down.

"You mean get into a fight?" she shrugged. "Sure, all the time. By the way, are these two your dogs?' she asked. "I'm sorry, but dogs aren't allowed in here, I'm afraid."

"Have you ever heard either one of them threaten each other?" Millicent, wanting to continue the interrogation, ignored her comment about the presence of Holmes and Watson.

"Silke pretty much tolerates all of his sputtering and spewing," she answered, "except when he starts calling her names. That's where she draws the line. Say, why are you asking me all of these questions? Are you the police or something?"

Alfredo calmly but seriously looked her in the eye. "As a matter of fact, we're private investigators, hired by FIFA to look into a private matter between Felix Fuchs and the police."

"Crap," the girl blurted, "that doesn't sound good at all. Hang on a minute and I'll go get Silke."

As soon as the counter girl left to retrieve her boss, Millicent quickly whispered for Alfredo to unleash both Holmes and Watson. "Let's see if the boys pick up on anything while we're waiting, shall we?"

"That's not a bad idea," he said, setting them loose. "Perhaps they'll be able to detect something that we or the police may find useful."

Millicent bent down as best she could and scratched behind both dog's ears. "My good boys," she said, "now, time for you to go search." And off they went, following wherever their noses took them.

It didn't take long, however, before the other ladies in the studio began to notice Holmes and Watson going about their business.

"Oh, looky here," a middle-aged woman on the elliptical machine said. "Isn't he the cutest thing you've ever seen?"

Instantly, Holmes stopped what he was doing and looked up at the woman. "Is she referring to me, dear Millicent?" he asked.

"Most assuredly," she answered.

The woman on the elliptical machine paused what she was doing to get a closer look at the cute, chubby dog now staring at her from the middle of the studio. "Does he have a name?" she asked.

"Why yes," Millicent answered. "He goes by Holmes, and the little black one over there, his name is Watson."

"Holmes and Watson, how clever!" the woman exclaimed as she sat down next to Holmes. "Aren't those the cutest names ever?"

Holmes raised his small chin proudly to allow the woman to stroke his bristly fur and rub his soft, tiny ears.

Soon the other two women in the studio cornered Watson, who by this time thought the ladies were playing chase with him, and so he continued to scamper about, making little yipping noises as he avoided their capture.

Soon Holmes was on his back, purring loudly as he enjoyed the massage his newfound friend was giving him.

"Well, so much for that," Millicent said as an aside to Alfredo. "We may have some trouble getting those two out of here when it's time to leave."

"Sì, Holmes and Watson are far too easy to tempt," Alfredo remarked. "And who can blame them."

Millicent couldn't help but giggle. "Certainly not me," she said. "Otherwise, I wouldn't have come all this way merely to take advantage of Helmut's magical, massag-ical fingers."

"What's going on in here?" a stern voice suddenly commanded. "How is it that these dogs are in my studio?" she asked, staring at Holmes and Watson before turning her glance toward Millicent and Alfredo. "And who are you people?"

Immediately, Alfredo introduced Millicent and himself before gathering up the pugs.

"And those two," she pointed out, "are my canine assistants, Holmes and Watson, respectively," Millicent answered as Alfredo leashed the boys back up one of the time. "We were hoping to have a word with you, Frau Schlumpf."

"You aren't police, obviously," she said. "So what are you? Private investigators?"

"Well, yes," Millicent answered hesitantly. "As a matter of fact we are."

"I'll have you know I run a perfectly legal business here," Frau Schlumpf exploded. "I have all the documentation to prove it, and my taxes are fully paid up to date."

"I'm sure they are," Alfredo quickly asserted. "We've not come here about your business, Frau Schlumpf."

"That's correct," Millicent added. "Actually, the reason why we're here is to inform you that Felix Fuchs was found dead this morning."

The room went surprisingly quiet.

"That doesn't surprise me," Silke finally said. "What with that temper of his, he was a heart attack just waiting to happen."

"I regret to inform you, Frau Schlumpf, I'm afraid Herr Fuchs did not die of natural causes but was instead unfortunately a victim of murder."

Silke let out a huge barrel laugh. "That doesn't surprise me either. That man had more enemies than friends. And I doubt very much he had many friends either."

"Is there someplace more private where we can sit and have this discussion?" Millicent asked. "My knees are starting to get to me, and the backs of my shoes are chafing my heels. I tell you, this happens every time my feet swell. I'll be so glad when this baby finally decides that enough is enough."

"Of course, I understand. Please, follow me to my office. The rest of you get back to your workout. And you," she said looking at the young counter girl, "you need to get back to your post."

"Yes, Frau Schlumpf, I'll do just that," she said as she gave Holmes and Watson a quick wink and a sweet little wave good-bye.

***

As soon as she entered her office, Silke Schlumpf made a beeline for her desk chair. Only one other chair was left in the room, and Millicent immediately plopped into it, leaving Alfredo to casually move about the office and take in whatever caught his eye. Holmes and Watson meanwhile continued sniffing their way into every nook and cranny they could get there little push faces squeezed into.

"So what is it that I can do for you, Frau Martolini?" the woman asked, seating herself. "Surely you don't think I had anything to do with this."

In truth Millicent wasn't sure what she thought, but she knew better than to trust her first impression, so went about her questioning nonetheless.

"My husband and I are but in the early stages of our investigation," she explained. "And because your name is on file as having an altercation more than once with Herr Fuchs, we needed to introduce ourselves to you and see if you had any information that would direct us toward whoever the criminal may be."

"I see," she said, leaning comfortably back in her chair. "Felix and I started out as being friendly toward one another—after all, for many years he was my soccer coach. But to say that we were true friends would be stretching it. Not once but many times we had a difference of opinion, particularly when it came to which players he'd chosen as his starters and which would merely come off the bench."

"But surely," Millicent pressed, "that wasn't enough reason for you to fill out a police report."

"You're right. No, it wasn't. You see, Felix had a way about him that made many of the girls on the team uncomfortable, if you know what I mean."

"Could you be a little more specific?" Alfredo asked, writing once again in a small notebook.

"Plain and simple, Felix was a womanizer," she continued. "He either flirted inappropriately with the girls on the team, or, like myself, made fun of them."

"Can you describe for me a specific instance?" Millicent asked.

"I can describe hundreds of instances, but here are just a few." She stood up and began to circle her desk, while at the same time keeping a watchful eye on Holmes and Watson.

"If he thought you were lazy, he pointed it out in front of the entire team. If he thought you are overweight, he not only pointed it out to the team, but he called you a name like *Porky* or *Fatso* or my favorite," she sneered, "*Brunhilde*. And if he thought you swung for the other team, sexually that is, then he had plenty of names where that was concerned."

"That must've made you quite angry," Alfredo said. "Perhaps angry enough to physically attack him?"

Silke stopped in her tracks. "Unfortunately, in spite of the fact that he was a major pain in our collective asses, Felix was one hell of a great coach when it came to the game of soccer. So we put up with his shenanigans because we liked winning our games. But it didn't take long for me to realize the sometimes winning isn't everything," she said making her way back to her chair.

"However, not once did I ever imagine him dead. I just wanted him to change the way he treated us. And the only way I knew how to do that was to report him first to FIFA and then to the police."

"And did he change?" Alfredo asked again as he circled the room while taking in the various trophies and plaques on the wall, testifying to the many awards Silke had earned over time as both a soccer star as well as a bodybuilder.

Silke let out a long sigh. "Sadly no," she said. "We even appealed to his wife thinking that perhaps she had some influence over Felix's behavior, but we may as well have been whistling in the wind. What a worthless excuse for a wife she is."

Millicent perked up. "You're speaking about Friedl?"

"Ja, good old Friedl," she said sarcastically, "in all likelihood she and Felix must've drifted apart years ago, for she was never around for our practices, and not once did she ever come to any of our games."

Millicent took in that information but chalked it up as mere opinion on Silke's part. "And they never had any children?" she asked curiously.

"That's a good one," Silke said. "The way Felix spoke about her, I doubt they'd ever once in their so-called marriage slept together."

"Not to change the subject or anything," Alfredo said, "but these awards of yours are extraordinary. How heavy of a weight do you usually bench press?"

"Oh, well, thank you," she said, brightening up a bit. "Ja, I've worked hard over the past few years to improve my strength and quickness. This morning in fact I actually pressed a little over sixty-five kilograms."

Alfredo whistled. "And your most recent dead lift weight?" he asked.

"The most I've ever dead lifted was twice my weight, about one hundred and eighty two kilograms. Usually, however, I lift less than that without breaking too much of a sweat."

Millicent struggled to get out of her chair, and with Alfredo's help she was soon on her feet, reaching over to shake Frau Schlumpf's hand. "I think that will be all of the questions we need to ask of you for now," she said with a smile, "but as we work on this case, we may need to do some follow-up. We only ask that you stay in town in case we need to contact you again."

"Of course, I understand," she said, heartily returning Millicent's handshake. "I hope you find Felix's killer soon so I can at the very least thank the murderer for doing what I've been too smart and too chicken to do myself."

Millicent thought the request through, and after a few seconds ultimately decided that it would be best to leave without comment. She then led Alfredo along with Holmes and Watson from the office, through the studio proper, and out the front door. It wasn't until they all reached the bottom of the outdoor staircase that either of the four said a word. Finally, she spoke. "Well, I don't know what I imagine, but that was totally unexpected."

"I agree," Alfredo said. "I don't know if you've noticed this or not, darling, but it appears to me that both Felix and his wife were not particularly well-liked."

"I know," she said, "and not only were they disliked by others, but it appears they didn't particularly like each other either."

Hanging on to Alfredo for leverage, Millicent bent over to speak to her canine assistants. "Holmes, Watson," she whispered, "did you pick up on anything while you were roaming the studio or Schlumpf's office?"

"I'm sorry to say that I did not, madam," Holmes answered. "In fact, thus far I haven't picked up on any scent comparable to what I discovered at Mozart's Geburtshaus."

"Yeah, me neither," Watson added, hopping from one clump of grass to another. "Could we please leave now? I'm so 'ungry I could eat me tail. Or better yet, 'olmes's. It's fatter."

The Case of the Magic Fluke

"There you go with your insults once again," Holmes barked out in return. "I'll have you know that my curly, cinnamon-roll-shaped tail is a work of perfection unlike yours, which looks like a stale, three-day-old bratwurst."

"That's enough you two," Alfredo announced. "I may be wrong, Millicent darling, but I think Holmes and Watson are feeling a bit peckish."

Millicent giggled. "I believe you're right, Alfredo. And if the truth were known, my stomach is growling again as well."

"The best thing then for us to do is make our way to that lovely little Italian restaurant we spied earlier and order our favorite dishes. Then we discuss what we know about the case as far."

"That sounds absolutely brilliant," Millicent agreed, already imagining all the lovely dishes she loved and missed since leaving Venice.

Even though the day had moved into evening, the sky was still lit by the sun as it made its downward journey behind the Northern Limestone Alps nearby. The temperature was likewise cooling down to a comfortable pleasantness as the four trotted where their collective stomachs were leading them—to food, glorious food.

***

It was true. Alfredo was all too aware that Millicent's brain worked so much better when she was consuming her favorite mealtime offerings, and particularly so when those dishes were laden with either mountains of pasta or stacks of sugary sweetness. And gratefully, tonight's bill of fare was comprised of exactly that.

Alfredo opened the door of the restaurant and immediately a tsunami of aromas wafted toward Millicent, propelling not only her but the others as well to float into the restaurant proper.

"May I help you?" the maître d'—a short, corpulent, pencil-thin mustached man—asked.

"Sì," Alfredo immediately answered. "We'd like a table for four please—hopefully, somewhat away from the rest of your guests."

"I have a table for two over in the corner. Will that do?" The maître d' pointed to a small table next to a large paned-glass window on the other side of the room. "*I tuoi piccolo carlini* can eat at your feet out of two small bowls I will be happy to provide for you."

"Will that work for you, *mia cara*?" Alfredo asked, but Millicent didn't hear him, for she and the pugs were already halfway to their designated table. He then turned to the man in charge and grinned. "*Si, grazie Signore.* My wife obviously finds your suggestion to be *assolutamente perfetto.*" The maître d' followed Alfredo close behind as the two gentlemen sauntered toward the table where already Millicent, Holmes, and Watson were already stationed.

"Oh, Alfredo," Millicent gushed, "isn't this the most exquisite

The Case of the Magic Fluke

Italian trattoria you've ever dined at? I mean, look at this lovely white linen tablecloth. And the design on this authentic ceramic dinnerware is elegance itself."

Alfredo was beyond pleased that Millicent found such pleasure in the simplest of things. "Sì, my darling, whatever makes you happy makes me happy too."

The maître d' quickly handed menus to both Alfredo and Millicent and told them the waiter would be at their table momentarily to take their order.

"So what looks good to you, *mia cara?*"

"My goodness, but everything looks so bloody good," she said enthusiastically. "Honestly, Alfredo, I don't know where to begin. Would you mind terribly ordering for the two of us?"

"Of course, Millicent. Your wish is my command."

"Oh," she said, nearly interrupting him, "and don't forget to order enough to feed the boys as well."

Within milliseconds the sound of two dogs yipping emanated from under the table near their feet as Holmes and Watson waited impatiently for the meal of their lives.

***

Millicent didn't realize she was as hungry as she was until she started eating, and then she became ecstatically aware that she was eating for two.

110

Cunigunda *Valentine*

First arrived the antipasto. Alfredo had ordered one of his favorite dishes, *Brischetta con Buratta et Acciughe.* Millicent also loved the bruschetta and the creamy Veronica cheese, but quite frankly could do without the anchovies. She, of course, would never tell Alfredo that, and not because she was afraid of hurting his feelings. No, the reason why she remained mute was because she knew how much Holmes and Watson enjoyed them. It was always great fun to sneak the anchovies away from Alfredo, one tiny fish at a time, and drop them on the floor beneath the table. And tonight was no different than any other night.

Next came the primo or what the Italians consider the pasta dish. Again Alfredo had ordered one of his favorites, *Cacio e pepe*, which was basically a type of nested spaghetti covered in a tangy sauce made of pecorino cheese and a whole lot of pepper. This was not as easy for Millicent to sneak to the boys, but she did nonetheless. Within seconds a barrage of sneezies emanated from under the table near Alfredo's feet.

"I hope you're not sneaking food to the boys, Millicent," Alfredo scolded with a twinkle in his eye. "I already ordered them a *pizza con salame*, which should be here any minute."

Millicent did her best to look innocent as she batted her eyelashes. "I would never do such a thing," she said, fingers crossed. "I know you have your rules, Alfredo."

She then smiled at him, knowing full well that he knew exactly what

111

she'd been doing, and, darn, if he didn't smile back.

"It's not that I have rules, *mia cara*," Alfredo said lovingly. "I know you well enough by now. You'd rather give the pugs your food than eat it yourself, but now is not the time with the baby nearly due to deny yourself this nutritious food."

As if on cue a small sized pepperoni pizza arrived at their table. Alfredo immediately cut it into small pieces and placed it at his feet. "Here you go, *miei amici*. Dinner is served."

Knowing how thirsty Holmes and Watson must be getting by now after having eaten all that black pepper, Millicent poured some of her water into her saucer and set it next to the chair by her feet. She smiled as she listened to the symphony of ecstatic slurps of Holmes and Watson.

"They seem to be enjoying themselves once again, *sì*?" Alfredo teased, causing Millicent to giggle.

"Tee- hee-hee," she answered back, "I wonder how can you tell," which in turn caused Alfredo to chuckle.

People in the restaurant seemed at first to be aware of a strange noise coming from where the Martolini's sat, but because they couldn't see anything unusual or out of place, they merely went back to their meals unaffected.

Just as Alfredo and Millicent finished the Primo course, on came the secondo, or what Italians refer to the meat or protein dish. Once again

Alfredo had ordered one of his and Millicent's favorites—*polpette*, or small meatballs, in marinara sauce. Normally, she could eat a dozen or more of these tasty morsels, but for some reason or another she was beginning to feel quite full.

"How are you doing, darling?" Alfredo asked, noticing her waning appetite. "Is everything all right?"

"Yes, of course, Alfredo," she said, and she meant it. "I think, however, I'll skip dessert for now."

"But tiramisu is your favorite."

"True, but I don't think I can eat another bite," she said, nearly groaning. "It's difficult enough for me to walk without being stuffed, but after tiramisu, it's nearly impossible. Besides, the walk will do us all good after the day we've had."

"Good thinking, my dear. Shall we go?"

"Yes, let's."

Millicent leashed up Holmes and Watson while Alfredo paid the bill. Soon they were out the door and on their way back to the hotel and the soft inviting comfort of their beds.

Chapter 8

It wasn't clear to Millicent if the reason why her energy level was changing was due to the fact that she was more active than usual, but something indeed was happening to her. She could feel it from her toes to her nose. It was like she had this boundless energy—all she needed was to go after whatever was on her mind and it would somehow magically be accomplished.

Maybe it's just the Italian food. Or perhaps it's that I've once again fallen off the pretzel wagon.

Millicent often equated her mood with food. It'd started when she was walking home from the restaurant. The closer she got to the hotel, the more she felt rejuvenated, unstoppable, alive. Not once did she think about her sore feet, or her cramping back, or her tired legs. Her major motivation was just to get back to the hotel and relax, take bubble bath, and perhaps watch an hour of *The Voice of Germany*.

In any case, Millicent and her retinue arrived at the hotel just in time for Reinhardt Rauscher, the hotel concierge, to tell her someone had phoned for her while she was out, and that he'd written down the number on a piece of paper and placed it in her resident mailbox.

"Alfredo," she said, "would you mind taking the boys upstairs to our suite? I want to call this number and see who it is before I take off my shoes and get into my nightie."

"Of course, my darling," he said lovingly, "it would be my pleasure."

Holmes and Watson also noticed that Millicent and Alfredo were in much better moods as compared to earlier that morning.

"Wassa 'nightie, 'olmes?" Watson asked.

"Millicent's night dress—you know that," Holmes answered

"I know," Watson giggled. "I was just testing you."

Holmes rolled his eyes.

Millicent then asked for a private area where she could make her phone call. She didn't recognize the number as belonging to Mr. Smythe, or the Salzburg Police Department, or Inspector Prachi Pesseingimpel's mobile. But being the adventurer that she was and feeling in high spirits, she decided to take a chance and see who was on the other end of the line.

The phone rang and the voice of young woman answered. "Hallo?"

"Yes, I'm Millicent Winthrop, and I understand you called the hotel earlier asking for me?"

"Oh, yeah," the young woman said, "as soon as you left, I remembered something that may be of help to you."

"And who is it that I'm speaking with?"

"It's me Berta Bellingshausen. You know, the receptionist at the gym you visited this afternoon."

"Oh yes, of course," Millicent answered, "I remember you. Does this have something to do with Frau Schlumpf?"

"Not exactly," the girl said, "no. But it is about Felix Fuchs. Silke always threatened to join the team of his rival coach, **Hedwig Hafelfinger**, who I know for a fact never got along with Felix or his wife. It's not much of a clue, I guess, and I don't know what I personally really think about Felix, Friedl, or Hedwig, but I've heard talk in the gym, and so I felt that it was important enough for me to call you."

Millicent fished around in her tote for a pen and paper to write down her information—the name of the coach, the coach's phone number, and any other vital information Berta may have for her. She even wrote down Berta Bellingshausen's name and where she could be reached.

"Thank you so much for that information, Berta," Millicent said. "Alfredo and I and the boys will follow this lead first thing in the morning."

"All right," the girl said, "Oh, and if you would, please don't tell Silke

I called. She'll have a hissy fit, and I don't want to be on the receiving end of that."

"Certainly," Millicent agreed, "I completely understand. You have a good night. And thank you for your timely assistance."

"Super," Berta said, "you have a good night, too, and good luck tomorrow. *Tschüss.*"

"Thank you, *ciao*," Millicent answered.

***

Riding the lift up to her suite, Millicent wondered why she hadn't heard as yet from Inspector Pesseingimpel, but then again, she'd just seen the woman earlier that day and had to assume that either the inspector was too busy to check in or that was just the way things were done in Salzburg. As soon as she opened the door to the suite, Alfredo greeted her with a kiss.

"Were you able to make your phone call?" he asked.

"Yes, and you'll never guess who it was."

"The inspector?"

"No, guess again," she said.

"I really have no idea, Millicent. Maybe my sister, Cecilia?"

Millicent chuckled. "No, it was the girl from the gym. The one who greeted us at the desk."

"Really? And what did she want?"

"I'm not sure, other than to inform us that a local rival girls' soccer coach, a Hedwig Hafelfinger, also had issues in the past with Felix Fuchs and his wife."

"Perhaps we should check that out tomorrow."

"I think you're right. She gave me the woman's contact information, so we'll connect in the morning. Did the inspector call you by any chance?"

"Not that I'm aware of," Alfredo said. "Odd, isn't it, that she hasn't called."

"Hmm" was all Millicent could say.

Even though it was nearly time to go to bed, Millicent was still wide awake. She wondered what she was going to do or say the next morning in order to get an interview with the rival coach. Something told her to also get a hold of Prachi Pesseingimpel, but something also told her to refrain. She hated it whenever she found herself in one of these push-pull moods.

Yet she'd learned a long time ago that when she had these ambivalent feelings, she'd better pay attention to them. Often they led nowhere, but every once in awhile they ended up leading to some of her most important discoveries in regard to crime solving.

They were also useful whenever she went clothes shopping by helping her decide what to buy, how much to spend, and how much then to show off to Alfredo. She knew he'd never deny her a thing, but she liked having her own autonomy by keeping her purchases temporarily hidden along with how much she'd paid for them.

Stupid, I know, she thought, *but that's just the way I am.*

She and Alfredo then gave the boys their baths before offering them each a half an amaretto biscotti. Now tucked into their beds on the sofa, it was her turn to take a luxurious bubble bath and go over what she had learned that day regarding the case.

In short, the victim was loved by his wife Friedl but not much by anyone else. To put it bluntly, Felix Fuchs was a major pain in the ass. The question was who'd had enough of his shenanigans to warrant murder. So far their only suspect was Silke Schlumpf, and even though Alfredo thought she might be a likely candidate, Millicent was not yet convinced.

By the time she came out of the bathroom. Alfredo was lightly snoring, signaling to her that he'd just fallen asleep. So she crawled into bed and kissed him gently on the cheek, causing him to turn over and mumble something along the lines of *tiramisu.*

She then switched off the light, turned over on her left side, and closed her eyes. Within minutes she smelled the aroma of a Galois cigarette. She looked around and immediately saw a chubby, baldheaded man in a swimsuit lounging in a deck chair situated on a lovely beach strewn with colorful sunbrellas.

"Monsieur H (pronounced *ahsh*), is that you?" she asked the man wearing sunglasses and a wide-brimmed straw hat.

"Of course," he answered, "it is I, Monsieur H of the Paris Sûreté at your service."

Millicent looked down at herself and saw she was wearing a white and gold French one-piece maillot cut high in the legs and plunged low in the bodice. Her toenails were painted bright orange, and she likewise was wearing a wide-brimmed straw hat and classic Christian Dior sunglasses. She also discovered she was wearing lipstick, which she could only assume was likewise bright orange.

"Where are we?" she asked. "And what are we doing on this beach?"

The odd looking Frenchman blew several perfect smoke rings into the air before replying. "I decided since you and Alfredo were on vacation, that I too would take a holiday to the south of France. I love the Cote d'Azur, don't you?"

"I'm not sure," she answered. "I don't think I've ever been to the French Riviera before. Have I?"

"If you have, Millicent dear, it certainly wasn't with me. That I am certain. Now please sit down under my umbrella. No use getting a sunburn this early in our conversation."

Millicent lowered herself into the empty deck chair on Monsieur H's right and proceeded to apply suntan lotion to her arms and legs. At once she was surprised to notice that she actually had a waist. In other words, at this particular moment, in this particular dream, she couldn't possibly be pregnant. And strangely enough, her lower back wasn't bothering her one bit.

"So tell me," she asked, "why again am I meeting you here in St. Tropez?"

"Ah, oui," Monsieur H (pronounced *ahsh*) sighed, remembering the reason why he had summoned Millicent by intruding into her dream world. "I merely wanted to touch base with you regarding your investigation of the murder of your latest victim."

"Do you know who the criminal is?" she asked.

"What I know is unimportant. What is crucial, however, is that you remember that most people are not always who they appear to be, especially those who choose to commit crimes against others."

"I already know that, sir."

"Oui, I know," he continued, "but it is imperative that you continue to understand what I have just said as you go about solving this particular case."

"All right," Millicent agreed, hoping she didn't sound as confused as she felt. "I'll do my best to operate according to your wishes. By the way, what is that you're sipping on?"

"*Pardonnez-moi, madam*, I must have forgotten my manners. Would you care to finish my drink?"

"Oh my, yes, . . . er . . . oui. That would be very nice, thank you."

"Ah, *alors*, but may I kiss you first? You are after all looking very chic this afternoon in your bathing attire."

"Uh . . . I don't know."

Before she could get out of her chair and away from the little French detective, Millicent felt his lips crash down onto her own.

"Oh, *mia cara*," a man's voice said, "sleep well my darling. We have a busy day tomorrow."

Millicent opened her eyes and was stunned to see that the person kissing her was her very own Alfredo—not a slightly overweight baldheaded Frenchman, sporting a pencil thin mustache and smelling of stale cigarettes.

"Yes," she whispered, "until tomorrow. I love you Alfredo."

"And I love you too, *la mia piccolo mamma*."

***

The next morning Millicent made sure she was first to shower, and no one was more surprised than her to find little grains of sand floating out of her freshly washed hair on its final rinse.

Nowhere in the world did this all come from? she wondered.

But then again it wasn't unusual for her to find the most obtuse things on her person when waking up from either a nap or a full night sleep. Something in the back of her mind made her suddenly think of how nice it would be to have a holiday on the French Riviera, but that would have to wait until next summer after the baby arrived.

She had the entire suite all to herself as Alfredo had taken Holmes and

Cunigunda *Valentine*

Watson out for their morning constitutional. This meant the bathroom was all hers. Millicent had a routine and no matter where she was in the world, she tried to adhere to it. Shower, wash hair, dry hair, put on body lotion (particularly around her belly), cream her face with an SPF cream, add a little lip gloss, and she was set for the day.

She was about ready to begin, when her stomach started to growl. Not one to stand in the way of her appetite, Millicent called room service at once and ordered coffee for Alfredo, English breakfast tea for her, a basket of pastries, four perfectly soft-boiled eggs, several slices of Swiss cheese, freshly churned butter, various fruits in season, and a plate of prosciutto.

"That should take care of the four of us," she said out loud in an attempt to organize herself. She'd just gone back to the restroom to finish her toilet when Alfredo and the boys returned.

"Good morning, my darling," Alfredo said, unleashing Holmes and Watson from their leads. "It looks as though it's going to be another beautiful day here in Salzburg. In fact, it's warm already."

"I'm in the restroom, but I'm almost finished," she said, fudging a bit. "And I ordered room service. Our breakfast should be here momentarily."

She then heard Alfredo mumble something in the background, but since the hair blower was on full blast, she had no idea what it was. Realizing that probably no one could hear her either, Millicent began singing snippets of the Queen of Night's aria from Mozart's *The Magic Flute*.

The Case of the Magic Fluke

Now Millicent was a lot of things, but a singer was not one of them. Yet like most people who sing snippets from operas during their morning bathroom routines, particularly when their hand-held hair blower is doing its thing full blast, she sang at the top her voice and with gusto.

Finally, Alfredo stuck his head in the door. "Is everything all right in here?" he asked.

"Of course," she said cheerfully, "why do you ask?"

"Ah, no reason, *mia cara*," Alfredo said innocently so as to cover his initial concern. "You seem to be in good spirits this morning. Did you sleep well?"

Millicent sighed. "Yes, I think so," she said. "I did dream last night, however, but darn if I can remember much of what it was about. I've scratched my head for the last few minutes, and the only thing I've come up with is the phrase *people often aren't who they appear to be*. Isn't that the most peculiar thing to have stuck in one's brain?"

"Nothing surprises me about your dream life, dear Millicent," he said with a chuckle. He then kissed her lightly and gave her tummy a gentle rub. "You go ahead and finish. I'll wait out here in the sitting room with the boys for our breakfast."

"All right, Alfredo. I shouldn't be much longer now."

***

Alfredo had learned some time ago that when Millicent said it shouldn't be long now, what she really meant was that it would be at least another hour. Thankfully, she had ordered breakfast, which should arrive soon—much sooner, in fact, than the completion of her morning regimen.

Not wanting to wait around and twiddle his fingers, as it were, Alfredo decided to give Inspector Pesseingimpel a call. It was important, he reasoned, to check in with the young inspector and relay the information he and Millicent had gathered after having visited Silke Schlumpf yesterday afternoon. More importantly, Alfredo was curious as to where the inspector had disappeared, and why she had not checked in with them.

"What do you think, boys?" he asked Holmes and Watson, who were standing up on the back of the sofa looking out the window at the sun-sparkled Salzach River below. "Should I give Inspector Pesseingimpel a call or wait for Millicent?"

"'e's not really asking us a question, is 'e 'olmes?" Watson asked. "I could understand it if he truly wanted an answer from us, but even if 'e did, it's clear to me 'e doesn't understand a single word we say."

Holmes pulled his gaze away from the window and locked in on Alfredo. "I think he's merely trying to include us in conversation, while at the same time garner permission to make the phone call in Millicent's absence."

"Yeah," Watson echoed, "Millicent's absence."

Holmes sighed. "I wish he would make up his mind for himself and take the initiative. And I think Millicent wishes the same thing herself."

"Yeah, the same thing."

"Tell you what," Holmes continued, "let's let out a quick bark and wiggle our hindquarters to make him think we agree. Obviously the man needs a nudge, and a yip and a wag from the two of us should suffice."

Alfredo dialed the number Prachi Pesseingimpel's mobile and waited for her to pick up. After several rings her voicemail kicked in.

This is the cell phone number of Inspector Prachi Pesseingimpel.

I'm unable to take your call at this time.

Please leave a message after the beep.

I'll get back with you as soon as possible.

"Hallo, Inspector. This is Alfredo Martolini. Millicent and I may have some useful information for you regarding the Felix Fuchs case. Please call either one of us as soon as possible. Thank you."

No sooner had Alfredo hung up, but that the doorbell rang, signaling to the boys it was time to go bananas. Holmes and Watson leapt off the couch and began barking and dancing around the room in expectation of what their little push-face noses were telling them. Food was once again on its way.

Alfredo was hungry as well, and couldn't in his right mind chastise the two pugs for their over the top display. Besides, there was nothing more charming than to see with each bark the front legs of both Holmes and

Watson leave the carpet and dangle in the air.

"A moment please," he said to whoever was behind the door. "Calm

down, you two. *Calmati*. It's only our breakfast."

He then waited patiently for them both to settle down before opening

the door. Reinhardt Rauscher quickly rolled his cart into the room filled

with not only what Millicent had earlier ordered, but other Austrian

specialties as well. Alfredo had barely had time to tip the concierge and

send him on his way when Millicent suddenly appeared.

"What's all the racket about?" she asked jokingly. "It's only breakfast."

Unable to contain themselves any longer, Holmes and Watson raced

from one side of the room to the other in expectation.

"Let's see what we have here," she said coquettishly to the boys. "Eggs,

Danishes —and what's this I see?"

Alfredo, Holmes, and Watson gathered closely behind her. "Ah,

bacon!"

With that Holmes jumped up into the air with glee, Alfredo let out a

jubilant *bravo*, and Watson nearly passed out.

Chapter 9

As soon as they were finished eating, Millicent offered to clean up what was left of their breakfast so Alfredo could take a shower and get ready for the day. It also allowed her time to telephone the Hafelfinger woman and asked for an interview. Before doing so, however, Millicent did a Google search on her computer and discovered there was very little information about the rival coach. This seemed odd to her, but then again everything about the case felt odd.

I mean, a dead body in Mozart's piano? Come on.

Then again, she had to admit that it was the only clue she had at the moment and therefore had to be pursued. The boys were now once again resting on the sofa, their warm little bodies curled up into themselves. Now was as good a time as any for her to take out her mobile and punch in the number given to her on the slip of paper she now held in her other hand.

"Hallo, who ith thith?" a child's voice answered before Millicent could identify herself.

"Hallo, I'm Millicent Winthrop Martolini. Is your child sitter or your mother at home?"

No answer, except for the sound of the receiver being dropped on the floor and a child's voice calling out for her mother. "Ith for you momma."

In the background Millicent thought she heard an exasperated woman blurt out, "Why does everyone in the universe have to call me in the morning? Can't they see I'm up to my nose in breakfast and diapers?"

For a brief second, Millicent didn't know whether to stay on the line of hang up. In fact, she was just about to punch the *leave* button when a woman's voice, accompanied by a screaming baby, answered the phone.

"For the ninetieth time, I don't want any," she bellowed into the receiver.

"Please wait, don't hang up. My name is Millicent Winthrop, and I'm calling you as part of my assignment as a private investigator in the Felix Fuchs case."

"What case?" Two other children were now adding to the cacophony of background noises.

"I regret to inform you that your colleague, Felix Fuchs, was found murdered this morning. My partner, Alfredo Martolini, and I have been

129

assigned by FIFA to investigate this case, and so having been given your name as a possible character witness," (*she was not going to say suspect*) "I was wondering if I could have a few words with you. Preferably this morning."

"Heinrich, put that down and quit hitting your sister with your hippo on a stick. . . . . I'm sorry, did you say he was murdered?"

"Actually poisoned, then stuffed in Mozart's piano at the Geburtshaus museum."

"Well, what do you know? He finally got what was coming to him. . . . Hannah, put the eggs back into the refrigerator and close the door before they get broken."

Millicent was sure she heard giggling in the background. Then the sound of something hitting the floor in full force. *Ka-plop!*

"Hannah, I asked you to do something for me and you ignored me. Go to your room . . . . Sorry, the children are a bit wound up this morning, so I have to get off the phone immediately."

"I understand," Millicent said, horrified by what was going on at the Hafelfinger household. "Why don't I stop by your place and we can talk at your leisure?"

"That would indeed by helpful . . . . Heinrich, get that toy out of the kitchen now or it'll be taken away from you and not returned." At once the baby burst out crying once again. "Oh, please, Heike, please don't cry."

"Tell you what," Millicent interrupted, "I'll be at your door within the hour. Hopefully, we'll be able to talk then."

She then heard the phone receiver on the other end hit the floor, as Hedwig Hafelfinger gave chase to her five year old son. Luckily, however, Berta had given Millicent not only the woman's phone number, but her address as well.

Alfredo, having finished his toilet, walked into the sitting room and watched as she hung up her phone.

"What's on the agenda today, my darling?" he asked while towel-drying his hair.

My Goodness, he's absolutely adorable when his hair falls in disarray onto his forehead. She sighed.

***

Thinking she might be tired given her condition and all, Alfredo read her sigh as meaning exactly that. "Or we can stay here in the hotel for part of the day if you'd like to rest."

"I had the most amazing conversation with Frau Hafelfinger, Felix's rival coach, but I think it's much too far of a stretch to suspect her of any malfeasance," she said, quickly changing the subject. "The woman can barely keep her head above water at home raising three small children, let alone plan and execute a bizarre murder such as what we have here. Yet I still think it's worth meeting with her face-to-face to make sure. Heaven knows my hunches have been wrong before."

The Case of the Magic Fluke

"*Splendido*, then, let's go." Alfredo hitched up Holmes and Watson to their leads, and deciding not to drive himself, called for a taxi. They then waited near the door for Millicent to finish her third morning trip to the loo. "Are you ready to go on yet another adventure *i miei due piccoli carlini*?" he asked.

Both Holmes and Watson wagged their hind ends vigorously in answer.

"'oo's Mel's piss ants? Watson asked in an aside to Holmes. "And why doesn't Millicent think this woman hasn't any?"

"You must be completely barmy," Holmes announced, "for I don't understand a single thing you're asking."

"You're awfully shirty again today," Watson remarked. "Millicent used a big word I've never 'eard her use before, and I wondered if you knew what she meant. That's all."

"Say it again."

Watson spoke loudly and slowly so Holmes would have no excuse to not get it. "Meelll's pisssss annnnts!"

Holmes scratched his head with his hind leg before making a full circle in place. "Ah ha," he finally said with a chortle, "you must be referring to *malfeasance*, yes?"

"That's what I said," Watson retorted. "Mel's piss ants"

"You really take the biscuit," Holmes said, giggling now while rolling on the floor. "*Malfeasance* is a perfectly reasonable word meaning wrong-doing. I can't believe you didn't know that, you wally."

"Hey," Watson argued, "'oo you calling a wally?" He then charged angrily toward Holmes, surprising Alfredo who rarely if ever witnessed a physical display of disagreement between the two of them.

"Say, what's going on here?" he asked. "I suppose we're all somewhat stir crazy this morning, but there's really no need for you two to act out."

Both chagrined dogs plopped down on the carpet and hung their heads over the fronts of their paws. Watson was the first to speak. "I'm sorry Holmes."

"I'm sorry too," his brother answered.

"And I'm sorry also that we have to wait so long for Millicent to make ready, but we love her and part of the way we show love to one another is by being patient toward one another."

Watson lifted his head. "Holmes," he whispered, "do you think Alfredo is beginning to understand us when we speak?"

Holmes thought about it for a moment and then replied with a wink, "Yeah, understand us."

***

After gaining instruction from Reinhardt Rauscher, Millicent and company took a taxi to the Salzburg train station. It turned out that Hedwig Hafelfinger and her three noisy children lived in the nearby picturesque town of Hallein, about nine kilometers from their hotel.

What kind of a husband leaves his wife alone all day with three pre-school children and no help? she wondered.

Holmes and Watson had never been on a train before, so they were quite excited. And so was Millicent, of course. Anything was better than walking and putting herself at risk for tired feet, a sore back, and swollen ankles.

Once inside the passenger car, she decided that this was as good a time as any to give Inspector Pesseingimpel another call. But as soon as the woman's phone picked up, it went once again to voicemail.

"You have reached the private phone of Inspector Prachi Pesseingimpel. I'm unable to take your call right now, so if you would leave your name and number and a convenient time for me to return your call, I will do so by the end of the day. Thank you."

Beep.

This is absolutely maddening, thought Millicent, but she nevertheless went ahead and left her a message.

"Hallo, Prachi, this is Millicent Winthrop Martolini calling. If you would be so kind as to return my call as soon as possible, Alfredo and I have made some interesting discoveries which we would like to share. Hope to hear from you soon. *Ciao.*"

"Any luck?" Alfredo asked as he saw her put her mobile back into her tote.

"Not yet, but it hasn't even been twenty-four hours since we last saw her, so maybe she's too busy or tied up with another case to call."

"I don't like this silence on her part. Something doesn't feel right to me," he said, causing Millicent to wonder not for the first time that perhaps the inspector was ignoring them.

But for what reason? Could the inspector perhaps have something to do with the Fuchs's murder?

"I don't either, Alfredo," she said. "For now, though, let's concentrate our energies on Frau Hafelfinger and see what she has to share with us."

"*Assolutamente, mia cara,*" he said smiling, "of course, you're right."

***

Upon arrival in Hallein, Millicent and company once again called for a taxi to take them to the address Hedwig Hafelfinger had dictated per their earlier telephone conversation. The beauty of the town was not lost on its visitors. Situated on the southern stretch of the Salzach RIver, the quaint village homes and beautiful churches were mirrored in the water's reflection, giving the place a magical feeling of another time and place. Even the dogs were silent as the taxi motored its way up the striking hills above the town.

Eventually the small SUV stopped in front of a brand-new and most impressive -looking chalet wrapped in tall glass windows, cement details, and natural wood decor. Alfredo whistled appreciatively. "*Mamma mia,* this is really something," he remarked.

"Yes," Millicent added, "and not at all what I was expecting." It took several stairs to get to the front door—a huge wooden edifice with inlays of carved figures of salt miners expertly displayed—, so that by the time they got there, Holmes, Watson, and Millicent were panting.

Alfredo rang the doorbell, which sounded a great deal like the tune from Rogers and Hammerstein's musical, *The Sound of Music.* At once they heard the sound of little feet rushing toward the door.

"I've got it," one voice said.

"No, I've got it," another said.

"I said it first," the first voice said again.

"Thath not fair. You alwayth get the door."

"You snooze, you lose."

"Mama, Heinrich ith thaying mean thingth to me again." And now the child belonging to the second voice was sobbing much louder than the musical selection of the doorbell.

"Heinrich, please," a woman's voice said. "You know, it wouldn't hurt you just once to let Hanna have a turn answering the door."

At last the door swung open, and there stood a rather attractive woman, holding a baby on her hip and holding back two eager toddlers.

"You must be the private investigators," she said. "Please, come in."

Cunigunda *Valentine*

The interior of the house immediately gave Alfredo the sense of wealth and privilege. The furniture, festooned with what looked like hundreds of toys, was of designer quality. The huge wraparound couch was made of a beige leather, the dining room table with places for up to twelve diners was made of the same would and natural staying as that of the walls of the chalet, and the few rugs scattered over the ceramic tiled floors were artfully and intricately designed.

"Thank you so much for agreeing to see us today, Frau Hafelfinger" Millicent said. "I hope you'll allow Holmes and Watson to also enter your beautiful home. They are after all very good boys."

"Why yes, of course," the woman said, placing her baby girl into the baby swing, "please be seated. And please call me Hedwig." She motioned toward the couch. "Can I offer you some refreshment? Tea? Water perhaps?"

Holmes started to whine.

"I think we're all fine," Alfredo said, "all, that is, except dear Holmes. Perhaps he could have a small dish of water, if it's not too much trouble."

Hedwig glanced down at the heavy-breathing pug. "Yes, of course," she said, running to her kitchen sink. "Is he okay? He isn't going to die, is he?"

"No, no, no," Alfredo answered with a chuckle, "not to worry. He's a bit overweight and stairs tend to cause him to hyperventilate."

That, and of course, a room full of screaming children, thought Millicent.

The Case of the Magic Fluke

As soon as Hedwig left the living room to go to the kitchen, the baby in the swing began to cry. As if on instinct, Millicent went over to see to the baby by picking her up and walking with her a few steps away and back to try to calm her down.

Heinrich and Hannah seemed to be fascinated by Holmes and Watson and were surreptitiously moving into their space. Millicent gave Alfredo a worried look, which he all but dismissed by placing Holmes and Watson on his lap so as to protect them from unwanted little hands. Hedwig then gave him the saucer of water, which he used to show the two children how to best take care of dogs.

She then threw herself into a nearby arm chair and let out a rush of air. Millicent noticed an identical chair and so sat down with the baby next to her. "You certainly have your hands full," Millicent said.

"You're telling me," Hedwig said with a sigh. "They drive me crazy, but I love them to pieces." She smiled over at Millicent. "The baby's taken a strong liking to you, thank goodness," she added, noticing the child playing with Millicent's sunglasses.

"What's her name?"

"Heike, after my husband's mother," she said. "Looks to me like it won't be long and you two will be starting a family."

"Yes," Millicent said beaming, "our baby's due in but a few weeks, or maybe it's days—I somehow always seem to lose track."

"I know, after the first one, I gave up counting," Hedwig said with a giggle. "So, how can I help you?"

"It's about Felix Fuchs," she said *sotto voce* so the children with Alfredo couldn't hear. "He was found yesterday morning stuck inside Mozart's piano at the Geburtshaus. At first we thought he'd been murdered at the site, but it turns out he was poisoned somewhere else and later placed under the lid of the piano. I understand you and he have been rival coaches for several years now."

"And you wanted to know if it was me who killed him." It was a statement and not a question.

"Well, yes. We're looking at nearly everyone as possible suspects since we have so very few clues to go on," Millicent continued while rocking the baby in her lap.

"Rest assured, it wasn't me," Hedwig said. "I don't have the time, energy, or child care coverage to even attempt such a thing, though there have been times in the past where I did a time or two consider it. Felix was a fine player in his day, but not that great of a coach. Oh, yes, his team always won no matter what the competition or tournament, but given his issues with women, he was not to be trusted. I'm sure if you interview the girls on his team, they'll verify that."

"If you had to guess who might be the culprit, who would you say?" Millicent's new interviewing technique was to ask the direct question rather than hem and haw.

Hedwig shook her head. "That's a tough one. My first answer would be *just about anyone.* But that wouldn't be entirely true. Many of the girls put up with his routine because they want to be winners and have a chance to compete at the national level. Whereas the girls on my team simply want to play for the love of the game."

"And your husband? How does he feel about this situation?" Another direct question from Millicent.

"Hans isn't interested in sports. Between his job and the children, he has little or no time for such *foolishness,* he calls it."

"Would it be all right if we spoke to him?" Millicent hoped that perhaps Hedwig's husband might be a possible suspect, even though she knew she was clutching at straws.

"You could if he was around, but he's not. In fact, he's in the Faroe Islands right now working on a construction project for the government and has been there for several weeks."

Well, that shoots that idea out of the water.

Both women went silent for a few moments as they stared at Alfredo along with Holmes and Watson playing quietly with Heinrich and Hannah. "You know, I think your husband also has the touch. I can see that you'll both be wonderful parents."

"Thank you, Hedwig," Millicent said, her eyes moist with tears. Baby

Heike in the meantime had fallen asleep in her arms, so Millicent carefully laid her in her playpen so as not to wake her up. She then cleared her throat, only to sneeze a quick ah-choo and hiccup a short hiccup. "Back to your guess as to who may have murdered Felix."

"Hmm . . . if I were you I'd check into his relationship with his assistant coach, Gisela Gruber. Rumors have been around for years that they've been having an affair. Maybe since Friedl won't give him a divorce, the assistant got fed up and did him in. Besides, I believe she's some kind of Mozart historian and works part time at the Geburtshaus and some of the other Mozart museums. I don't know—it's just a guess."

Millicent's ears pinged, as did those of Holmes and Watson.

At last, a bona fide clue.

"Well, thank you for your time, Hedwig. I only hope I'll someday be able to manage both family and career as well as you have yours."

Hedwig, Heinrich and Hannah saw Holmes and Watson, Alfredo, and Millicent to the door. The children hugged the pugs one more time as Hedwig did Millicent. Upon Alfredo's suggestion the taxi had waited for the Martolini's to finish their interview before whisking them back to the train station where they had earlier been picked up. They'd no sooner arrived, when Millicent's mobile rang.

I hope to heaven this is the inspector, she thought as she fished around in her tote for her phone. She looked down at the number displayed on her phone. *Who in the world can this be?*

Chapter 10

Millicent hesitated before answering the phone. What she didn't need right now was a prank call, or worse, a telemarketer, trying to sell her the latest in household appliances or beachfront property in Wyoming. She had to admire their ingenuity, even though she found their tactics rather ridiculous.

"Hello, this is Millicent Winthrop. Who may I say is calling?"

"Oh Millicent" a sobbing voice said, "I hope I may call you Millicent. This is Friedl Fuchs. I was wondering if you could bring me up to date on the investigation of my dear husband's murder."

"Why yes, of course, Frau Fuchs," Millicent emphasized her name for Alfredo's benefit, "it's good to hear from you." Alfredo nodded.

"I've been so worried, what with this murderer on the loose. And no one seems to be able to give me any kind of answer. And please, call me Friedl. I must've called Inspector Pesseingimpel a dozen times, and I still can't seem to get through. Where is she, I wonder?"

"I have a call into the inspector and hope to hear from her soon," Millicent said, not wanting to upset the woman by mentioning that she'd had issues getting through to the woman as well.

"So, do you have any suspects at all?" Friedl asked.

"We've interviewed several people and are on our way to make contact with another shortly. Why? Do you know of anyone who might've wanted to do harm to your husband?"

"Only that idiot, Silke Schlumpf, and perhaps someone connected to soccer. You know, many professionals in the sport of European football have over the years been quite jealous of my husband's wins, of which there are many."

"I can imagine," Millicent agreed. "Alfredo and I did have a good conversation with Hedwig Hafelfinger, but soon realized that it would been logistically impossible for her to have done the deed."

In other words, she had an alibi?"

"I'd say she had three alibis, yes."

"Then I'm truly at a loss," she said, before going on a much louder and intense crying jag.

"Look, trust me Friedl. Alfredo and I along with Holmes and Watson are doing our best. You can be assured of that."

"I certainly hope so. I'm so counting on all of you to solve this horrible crime so I may grieve appropriately and one day with any luck move on."

"We understand, Friedl," Millicent said in an attempt to give her some kind of comfort. "If anything comes up in the next few days, we'll certainly get in touch with you. In the meantime, take care of yourself and try not to worry. Everything will turn out just the way it should. You wait and see."

***

By the time they arrived at the Hallein train station, the conversation had ended. "That sounded interesting," Alfredo remarked. "We don't often have missing police personnel and the spouse of our kidnapped or murdered victim calling us out."

"I know," Millicent said, "but she's right. The inspector is impossible to get a hold of, and our list of suspects is shorter than the time left of my pregnancy. I'm sorry, Alfredo, but I do feel somewhat guilty, like I haven't been up to my usual level of competency."

"I understand, my darling," Alfredo said, "but we are doing our best, and that's really all that counts."

"I guess you're right, but still. I truly do feel for the woman, for I don't know what I'd do if anything ever happened to you."

***

At once the train to Salzburg arrived. In less than 30 minutes they be back in Salzburg and ready to enjoy their favorite time of the day— lunch.

"I think I know what would make you feel better, my love," Alfredo said with a twinkle in his eye. "Let's go to the organic *Grünmarkt* delicatessen and pick out some cold cuts and cheese for a short picnic in a nearby park. How does that sound?"

Holmes and Watson pranced about in approval, causing Millicent to chuckle and briefly ease out of her less-than-happy mood. "Brilliant," she said and meant it.

Alfredo procured another taxi so that the four would still have energy enough to perhaps do some investigative work after a quick meal. He was particularly concerned about Millicent, for even though she was putting on a cheery face, he could tell that something had altered her ever so slightly. And the only thing he could point to was the telephone conversation she'd had with the Fuchs woman.

The minute they stepped out of the taxi, Holmes and Watson made a dash for the delicatessen, pulling Alfredo nearly off his feet. Luckily, Alfredo still had a hold of their leads, or the pugs most assuredly would've found themselves in all kinds of trouble. Particularly Watson, as he was known to be a confirmed sausage addict.

"Hold on a minute, boys," Alfredo said with a chuckle, "we've should wait until Millicent catches up. That way we can all order together." In the meantime, he picked out what he thought Millicent and the pugs would most enjoy—venison salami, smoked ham, and thick slices of cheese produced locally.

Millicent at last appeared holding along with her tote a bouquet of fresh cut flowers. "Sorry I'm a bit late. I saw these lovely blooms the moment I stepped into the market, and I knew then and there I had to have them. Aren't they beautiful?"

Holmes and Watson were too busy eyeing the refrigerated case to pay much attention to Millicent's flower purchase, and Alfredo was preoccupied in paying for his chosen selections for their afternoon Charcuterie.

"Oh my God," Millicent suddenly shrieked, causing the Alfredo, Holmes, and Watson in that order to jump back from what they were doing and stare at her in fright. "Would you look at those amazing pretzels?" she asked with amazement. "Why, they're as big as Holmes and Watson combined."

"*Mamma mia*, Millicent," Alfredo said, "you scared us half to death. I thought it was time for the baby to come."

Holmes sneezed in indignation at having been compared to a pretzel, while Watson merely giggled.

"Sorry, but you know how I am about my pretzels—the bigger, the better."

Alfredo hurriedly asked the man at the counter to include two pretzels with his earlier purchase, which the cashier gladly obliged. Then they set foot for the nearby park. Alfredo had inquired as to directions before Millicent's arrival.

"Fürtwangler Park—it's quite lovely, really. And there are benches for us to sit on while we enjoy *il nostro pranzo*.

What's 'e talking about, 'olmes?" Watson asked.

"Lunch, my dear fellow," Holmes answered. "One of my three favorite meals of the day."

Once the retinue cozied up onto the park benches, Millicent divided one pretzel into numerous small bites of the pugs, while Alfredo tore the other in half. The halves were slightly uneven, so Millicent laughingly snagged the larger of the two.

Alfredo pretended to be insulted. "Why do you always fight to take the bigger portion, darling? You know I'd gladly give it to you."

"When it comes to pretzels, Alfredo, I'm definitely eating for two."

***

Things became rather quiet as the four of them moved through their lunch. That was, except for the smacking of Watson's lips and the moans of appreciation from Holmes. After several minutes and fully sated from her half of the pretzel, Millicent at last spoke.

"Alfredo, I've been thinking about this new lead in the case—Miss Gisela Gruber. I know Hedwig was trying to help, but doesn't it seem odd to you that a woman would kill her lover just because he didn't want to marry?"

"Mmmmm, maybe," Alfredo puzzled, "but I think we need much more information and backstory about their relationship before we make any assumptions, sì?"

"Yes, I suppose you're right," Millicent said half-heartedly. "But before we go any further in our investigation, I think we need to talk. You're not going to like what I'm about to suggest, but I think this case warrants it."

Holmes and Watson momentarily stopped their eating and were all ears. Alfredo also ceased chewing, his mouth still full of salami. Unable to speak with his mouth full, he merely nodded.

"I think I should after all try to go into trance and see if I can put myself into the body of the criminal so as to get a better picture of how the murderer committed his or her crime."

Alfredo quickly swallowed his half-chewed food. "I thought we already agreed that you would not try this while carrying our child. You know as well as I that going into trance has always been dangerous for you, and now that you are with child, the very act of going deep into your psyche could be too much for the fetus. And you don't want to intentionally bring harm to our baby, now do you." Alfredo said the last sentence as a statement, not as a question.

"But if you were next to me, holding my hand and guiding me through the process, watching to make sure things don't get too real or too rocky, surely that would be safeguard enough. Don't you think?"

"No, I do not think," Alfredo clipped. "You promised me that should we could work during your pregnancy, you would take care not to put yourself or our baby in danger. Now you want to back out from your promise? No, Millicent, I will not allow it."

Millicent sighed. She knew Alfredo was right, yet she wanted to move forward with this case much more quickly and efficiently than they had the last two days. She also wanted to be of service to Friedl Fuchs, the Salzburg police, and to Mr. Smythe and FIFA. The truth of the matter was that she was totally unsure if she still had the ability to view in her mind's eye the crime as it was being committed from the viewpoint of the criminal. When she was at the height of her troublesome personality disorder, she could sink into one of her episodes at the drop of a dime. Easy Peasy. Now that she was on the mend, mentally speaking, she found the process to be much more intense, unreliable, and physically debilitating.

Oh, what to do?

"If it's all right with you then, let's contact Frau Gruber and see if we can get an interview with her today before we turn in. Agreed?"

"Sì, agreed," Alfredo said far too quickly for Millicent's taste. She could tell he was uneasy about her suggestion, and she didn't blame him one bit. How many times in the past had she promised him this, that, or the other thing but went ahead and did whatever she wanted. He'd always forgiven her, but now that the baby was in the picture, she wasn't so sure he'd be all that forgiving should she break her promise. Trust in a relationship was a fragile thing and should not be toyed with—this she knew.

But still . . . .

***

Alfredo's heart raced. *How can she even suggest such a thing?* He always forgave her unreliability when she was still dealing with her three distinct personalities. He had to, for she was so fractured at the time, that when one personality took over, the other two were totally at a loss as to where she was and what she was doing. From the outside, it looked like amnesia. Yet as he and his sister Cecilia began to understand the true nature of her situation, that she was not only Millicent Winthrop, but Veronica Nero and Kathryn Richards as well, then they were able to move her toward healing. The only remnant of those complex and convoluted days of psychosis was her continued ability to still speak with and understand what was spoken by Holmes and Watson—her therapy dogs, now canine assistants.

Yet trance or no trance, Millicent knew that their next move was to speak to Gisela Gruber to see if she might be their suspect, or at the very least, to ascertain any new information regarding possible motives for

Felix's murder, other than he was a first-rate pill to just about everyone except his wife.

"Rather than call first, Alfredo, I think it would be best if we drop by unannounced to Fräulein Gruber's place of residence. Obviously, the Geburtshaus is closed, as it is still a crime scene until everything's been processed, so she more than likely isn't there right now. And I doubt she's in the mood to do any kind of research at the library. So let's put our heads together and see if we can track her down."

Alfredo nodded and straight away took out his mobile to search for Gisela Gruber's address. "Here's a *G. Gruber* residing in an apartment close to us, as well as to Mozart's Geburtshaus. I bet you anything that's her," he said.

"Then let's go. I feel like taking a brisk walk after that humongous pretzel we ate. Is that okay with you two?" she asked Holmes and Watson.

"Indubitably," Holmes remarked, as he scrambled up onto his four stick-like legs and gave himself a shake.

Watson followed suit. "Yeah, indu . . . induta . . . er . . . what 'e said."

***

Alfredo grabbed the boys' leads, Millicent her tote filled with flowers, and off the four of them set for their next interview.

"Perhaps we should give Inspector Pesseingimpel a call to let her know where we are at in our investigation," he suggested.

"I doubt very much that she'll answer her mobile," Millicent said with a scowl. "I've tried several times over the last twenty-four hours and have had no luck. Why don't you try this time? Maybe she'll be more willing to strike up a conversation with you than she's been with me."

"If she doesn't answer, I'll at least leave a message on her voicemail, sì?"

"Please do," she said. "Even if she's not interested in following up this case, we at least must show our interest to the powers that be should there be an investigation into her dereliction of duty. I have a good mind to report that girl."

"*Calmati*, darling," Alfredo responded. "After all, it's only been shy of a full day since we've spoken with her. We need to remain patient, especially since we are but guests in this beautiful country."

"I suppose so," she said, between short intakes of breath. "How much further is her apartment house did you say?"

"I believe it's around this corner." Alfredo had a gift for finding addresses, which was a good thing since Millicent had no talent whatsoever in that regard.

When they arrived at the address, all four stood staring at the building, catching their collective breaths. Watson tinkled next to a light post, while Holmes sniffed around the entranceway.

The Case of the Magic Fluke

"What floor does it say her apartment's on?" Millicent asked.

Alfredo checked the mailboxes just outside the door. "Her apartment number suggests it's on the second floor. Are you ready for me to push the buzzer to see if she's in?"

"Please," she answered, taking one last deep breath before possibly having to manage the next two flights of stairs. "I wish they'd put more electric lifts into these old buildings."

"Ah, but then what would we do, other than walk, for our exercise, *mia cara*, Alfredo said gently. "Okay, now I'll let her know we are here."

Alfredo pressed the intercom button next to the woman's name and within seconds her heard a sad, soft woman's voice answer.

"Yes?" she asked.

"Hallo, Fräulein Gruber. This is Alfredo Martolini. My wife, Millicent Winthrop, and I are here as private investigators to ask you a few questions pertaining to Felix Fuchs. Would you be so kind as to give us a little of your time so that we can find out who it is that has murdered your dear friend?"

Millicent smiled. *Oooh, he's so good with people. Much better than me. No wonder the ladies love him,* she thought while listening in on their conversation. True to form, without saying a word the young woman straight away buzzed the four of them in.

They took their time climbing the stairs, until they were at last standing in front of the correct door. Alfredo knocked.

"Hallo, Gisela Gruber?" he asked.

"Yes, just a moment," she answered, "let me first get another tissue."

The door opened, and to their great surprise, the apartment was something out of *Architectural Digest Magazine,* the luxury apartment issue. The high-ceiling walls were painted a deep peacock blue, bordered by lovely wooden wainscoting in white. Above the fireplace in the small living room hung a huge, gold framed mirror, giving the illusion that the room was much larger than it actually was. In the corner next to the French doors leading out to the balcony stood a white, baby grand piano, above which hung a massive gold chandelier festooned with crystal beads.

From where Millicent stood she was unable to see either the kitchen or bedroom, but she imagined that they were just as opulent as the rest of the place. Eventually she knew she'd have to use the restroom, and so she promised herself that she'd give the apartment a good snoop at that time.

"Please come in," Ms. Gruber said, gesturing. "I'm afraid you'll have to excuse the way it looks. I haven't felt much like cleaning these last two days."

Other than a few used tissues scattered here and there, Millicent couldn't see a thing out of place.

"Your home is quite lovely, Fräulein Gruber," Alfredo said as he and the others moved in.

"Please, call me Gisela. Everyone does," she said as she blew her nose.

After perusing the woman's apartment like the PI that she was, Millicent noticed how unkempt Gisela appeared. Her face, particularly her eyes, was red, and her hair uncombed. Even her sweater was buttoned wrong. Over on the piano sat a saucer holding a half-eaten sandwich of bread and cheese.

"I hope we haven't disturbed your lunch," Millicent said, referring to the saucer.

Gisela merely stared in the direction of the piano. "Oh, yes, that was supposed to be this morning's breakfast, but I'm afraid I don't feel much like eating. But, please, excuse my manners. Won't you be seated?"

"Grazie Gisela," Alfredo said, leading Holmes and Watson to sit on the floor next to him. He and Millicent gratefully sat on the blue-and-gold brocaded sofa and waited for Gisela to lower herself into the matching side chair.

"We are indeed sorry for your loss, Gisela," he said, "and we would be remiss to not give you the time you need to grieve, but we have an assignment to fulfill, and that is to find who it is that murdered your dear friend and colleague. I'm sure you understand."

"Yes, of course," she said as if in a daze. "I'm surprised that you're here, for yesterday I answered as many questions as one could possibly be given by one Inspector Prachi Pesseingimpel."

Alfredo and Millicent suddenly looked at one another.

"Really? The inspector came to see you yesterday?" Millicent asked.

"Yes, she came by to give me the news of Felix's murder and to see if I had any idea who would do such a thing." Once again tears slowly formed in Gisela's eyes and rolled down her cheeks.

"At first she made it clear that I was under suspicion due to my relationship with Felix, as well as my part-time job at the Geburtshaus. I told her as I'm now telling you I would never hurt anyone, least if all the man I'd promised to marry as soon as he was free from his marriage."

Millicent felt her own eyes fill with tears. Both women now blew their noses simultaneously.

Damn hormones. Hiccup. Ah-choo. "Pardon me," Millicent said, followed by a moment of silence. Finally, Alfredo spoke.

"Do you think that you may have been framed, Gisela?" he asked gently.

Gisela gave her nose one final honk. "There are certainly enough people I wouldn't put it past."

"Like who?" Millicent asked, drying her eyes.

Gisela leaned back and sighed. "The list is too long to repeat, but give me just a minute to recover, and I'll do my best."

Chapter 11

Alfredo took out his notebook and pen, readying himself for what Gisela Gruber was about to reveal. Without a moment's hesitation she proceeded to list all the women's professional and semi-professional football managers and their assistants within the entire country of Austria. She went through them so quickly, in fact, that Alfredo could hardly keep up. In other words, he put his pen down and merely listened.

Millicent wasn't near as patient. "But Gisela," she interrupted, "are you sure all these people wanted to see Felix dead or just merely to be bested?"

"That's a good question," she answered. "Many of them became better coaches by observing Felix's technique. I also think most of them secretly wished they could be as good at winning as Felix, but jealousy makes good people sometimes do bad things."

Millicent thought that through for a moment, but then continued with her questioning. "How about the girls on his team? Do you think any of them might have wanted to see him dead?"

Gisela sighed before answering. "I think they all must have at one point or another wanted to do him some kind of bodily harm. After all, Felix was tough on the girls. He had them practicing hard every day without fail, no matter what the weather or excuse. And he didn't put up with any nonsense, either."

"He sounds tough," Alfredo inserted.

"Yes, but I think most of the girls respected him for it, for he was always right out there with them on the pitch, doing the exercises and drills they'd all grown to hate but understood how they made them better players."

"And how about you, Gisela? Did you ever want to see him dead?"

"Never ever, not even once," she answered firmly. "After my knee injury, Felix gave me a chance to prove myself as an assistant coach. And he was as tough on me as he was on the others. More so at times. But I would not have become the person I am today without his tutelage and mentorship. I owe him everything."

She now broke down into a sob. "He was my everything. And I will miss him more than you'll ever know."

The Case of the Magic Fluke

Alfredo handed her one of his ever-available clean white handkerchiefs, which she used to cover her face as she let go of her sadness.

"One last question, and then we'll leave you alone," Millicent said tenderly. "What did his wife, Friedl, think of your relationship with Felix?"

"Oh, that horrible woman," she said, coming up for air. "She wouldn't let Felix go, in spite of the fact that she already had another lover."

Millicent gasped. This was not the answer she'd expected, especially after her conversation earlier that morning with Friedl concerning the investigation.

"And do you know who that person might be?" she asked cautiously.

Gisela blew her nose once again, only this time into Alfredo's hanky. "Of course, I know. Felix did too, as well as everyone else around here connected with football— their neighbor, Tobias Tichendorff."

***

The Martolini's along with Holmes and Watson swiftly offered their *Auf Wiedersehens* and hurried out the door.

"The case gets more and more convoluted with each step with take," Millicent said, grateful that she was going down stairs for a change rather than huffing and puffing going up.

Alfredo had to agree. "I'm of the belief that some people are lying to us," he said. "And I'm still uneasy about our vanishing inspector."

"Yes, but who is the question."

Alfredo released a breathy *ho*. "You know, when I was practicing psychotherapy, I had the same feeling—that my clients from time to time lied to me, especially in the first few sessions."

"Why do you think that was?" Millicent asked, curious as to why anyone seeking help would do such a thing.

"I'm not sure, but I believe it was for one of two reasons. Either they wanted me to like them so I'd continue as their therapist, or they were attempting to cover up something they did not want me to know about. In any case, it eventually became clear to them that healing would not be possible as long as they were being dishonest."

"I see," she said. "So the question now is who of our suspects has the most to profit from being dishonest."

"*Esattamente.*"

"Exactly," she translated.

But who? The question tumbled around in her brain until she could not longer think. *And why won't Alfredo trust me enough to allow me one measly episode?*

Her silence must have bothered Alfredo as much as it did Holmes and Watson, for all three started chattering at once to fill the gap in the conversation.

Holmes began by clearing his throat. "Madam, may I suggest that we go through the list of possibilities, not matter how far-fetched, and see

161

if anyone stands out."

"Yeah," Watson agreed, "stands out."

"I may be incorrect, darling," Alfredo added, "but I think what the boys are suggesting is that we carefully examine each person that we've met thus far and ask ourselves if that person may be indeed our killer."

Millicent agreed. "All right then. Let's go ahead and stroll back toward our hotel. I know myself well enough that once we've had this talk, I'm going to need to lie down for a bit before dinner. I think all this running around is beginning to get to me."

As they walked, Alfredo took Millicent's hand in his. "Let's begin with Walter Winckelmann."

"Who's he again?"

"The docent at the Geburtshaus who we met first thing yesterday. You remember."

"Oh, yes. Of course," she said, bringing the figure of the old man into her mind's eye. "I don't for a minute think it was him. Do you?"

"Not at all," he agreed. "First of all, he may have means as he's in charge of opening and closing the museum, but he has no motive and from what I can tell, little or no upper body strength."

"All right, next."

"The illusive Inspector Prachi Pesseingimpel—what's your opinion regarding her?" he prodded.

162

"I have no problem with how she handled the early investigation of the case. And I haven't the foggiest as to what if any motive she may have at murdering Herr Fuchs. In fact, the only thing that bothers me about her is how difficult it is to reach her by phone."

Holmes was not about to be left out of the conversation. "Do you think, my dear," he asked, "there's any possibility she could be a dirty cop?"

"Yeah," Watson echoed as usual, "dirty cop."

Millicent was aware that both pugs had seen far too many BBC detective programs on the telly and thus figured perhaps that may be coloring their thinking.

"I don't believe the inspector is dirty, but I suppose there's always that chance," she said.

"And then there's Silke Schlumpf," Alfredo said, moving the discussion along, "along with her receptionist, Berta Bellingshausen."

Millicent reflected on yesterday's visit with the woman and her assistant. "So far she does seem to be our most likely candidate."

"Because she had motive, or at least history with the man, as well as means," Alfredo said. "She's certainly strong enough to kill any man, and with Berta's help they could easily have transported him to the Geburtshaus."

"But how did they get in without a key? There's no sign of a break-in. And I checked before leaving—the door locks from the outside, but the keys were still hanging in the office by the time we got there."

"You're right, *mia cara*. So that brings us to Hedwig Hafelfinger."

"Well, she certainly had motive, but there's no way she could have logistically pulled it off. Not with three kids and an out-of-town husband."

"So that brings us to Gisela Gruber," Holmes added. "She may easily have had motive as well as means— at least she more than likely has her own set of keys for the Geburtshaus. But I'd be hard pressed to think she has the strength to move a dead body."

"Yeah, a dead body," Watson said, nodding his head in agreement.

"And I have to say that I believed Fräulein Gruber was telling the truth," Millicent added as the four crossed the bridge over the Salzach River, their hotel in sight. "That she honestly loved Felix and hoped to have a future with him once he was divorced."

"So why kill him?" Alfredo asked.

"Why, indeed."

"You haven't as yet mentioned the wife, Friedl Fuchs. If what Gisela told us was the truth, she certainly had motive—perhaps the strongest and most believable thus far—yet how could she have maneuvered Felix's body into the Geburtshaus by herself?"

Holmes cleared his throat once again. "Perhaps she *wasn't* by herself," he said, "perhaps she had help from Inspector Pesseingimpel."

"Yeah, Pesseingimpel."

"Or this neighbor of hers, Tobias Tichendorff." Holmes was on a roll.

"Yeah, Tichen— what?" And Watson, as usual, was not on a roll.

"Tobias Tichendorff," Millicent blurted, "remember Gisela hinted that Friedl may be having an affair with this man, and if that's true, it would mean she'd have easy access to an accomplice—someone to help her with her husband's body."

"Sì, but what about the keys to the Geburtshaus? Alfredo asked. "How is it she had those?"

Millicent stopped dead in her tracks, causing everyone else to do the same. "Alfredo," she said, "please phone Gisela right this minute and ask her if she has a set of keys for the museum. And ask her if they happen to be missing."

Alfredo handed off the dogs' leads and stepped a few feet away from Millicent to make the call. Not one to mistake an opportunity whenever it appeared, Millicent bent down to speak to Holmes and Watson, who were sitting on their haunches, ready to listen to whatever she had to say."

"One more interview, boys, and then we can have our dinner at the hotel. Our best clue yet is this Herr Tichendorff, who we must apprehend quickly before he's on to us and takes off. So be patient. I have a feeling this case is about to finally be wrapped up."

Millicent noticed that Alfredo had a grin on his face as he turned back toward her. "You are a genius, my darling," he said. "Gisela does indeed have keys to the Geburtshaus, and, surprise-surprise, they've been missing for the last few days."

"Then we must speak immediately to Tobias Tichendorff and find out what he has to say regarding his involvement in this case."

Alfredo at once looked up the man's contact information, particularly his phone number, and gave it to Millicent. Without waiting a second longer, she punched the number into her mobile. Meanwhile, Alfredo looked up the man's address along with that of the Fuchs and called for a taxi.

She waited two rings before a man's voice spoke into her phone, identifying himself as Tobias Tichendorff.

"Hallo, Herr Tichendorff. This is Millicent Winthrop. My husband, Alfredo Martolini, and I are private investigators from Venice, Italy, assigned to the Felix Fuchs murder case. Might we trouble you for a few questions about your neighbor?"

The line was silent save for the sound of a man breathing quite heavily in the background.

"Herr Tichendorff, are you still there?"

"*Es tut mir leit*, but I think you must have the wrong phone number," the voice said.

"No, I don't think I have the wrong phone number—and neither do you Herr Tichendorff. How long have you and Friedl Fuchs had an intimate relationship?" she asked directly, as was her habit.

"I don't know what you're talking about," he stammered.

"You know, your neighbor—Frau Friedl Fuchs—the woman you assisted in murdering her husband."

"Look, I don't know where you're getting your information, but you can't stalk innocent people like myself and expect to get away with it."

"I'm not trying to get away with anything, Herr Tichendorff. Are you?"

"That's it," he yelled into the receiver, "I'm reporting you to the police right this very moment."

The line went dead.

"He hung up on me," Millicent announced. "Come on, we've got to get over to his house now."

The taxi Alfredo had called pulled up just as Millicent pocketed her phone in her tote. He and the boys limbed into the back seat while Millicent slid into the front. Alfredo then gave the driver Tischendorff's address and ordered him to make it snappy. "*Per favore presto*," he said, "it's a matter of life and death."

***

As soon as Tobias hung up on Millicent, he straight away punched in a phone number he'd called many a time and knew by heart. And it wasn't that of the police.

***

All the way over to the Tichendorff home Millicent worked at trying to get a hold of Inspector Pesseingimpel one last time, but as usual had no luck.

"It's as if she's disappeared off the face of the earth," she said to Alfredo and the boys. "I can't tell if she's in trouble, or involved in this thing illegally, or just plain lazy. But I've had enough of this nonsense. I'm calling the police."

"I would say that it's about time we did so, darling," Alfredo agreed. "I have to admit that this behavior of hers is extremely odd and may after all have everything to do with our case."

Millicent spared no time at all in ringing the emergency number of the Salzburg Police Department. "Good afternoon," she began, "I'd like to report a missing person."

She listened as the call was being transferred, and a new person came on the line. "Missing Persons, can I help you?"

"Of course," she said calmly, knowing her patience was being tested, "I'd like to report a missing person of interest in regard to the recent murder of Felix Fuchs."

"And the name please?"

"Mine or the missing person?" she asked, temporarily confused.

"Let's begin with yours."

"I'm Millicent Winthrop of the Winthrop-Martolini Private Investigation business out or Venice, Italy, and the person I'd like to report missing is Prachi Pesseingimpel."

"Wait . . . what? Our Inspector Prachi Pesseingimpel?" the voice asked incredulously.

"Yes, the one and the same."

***

The taxi at last pulled up in front of the Tichendorff residence. Alfredo looked to his left and instantly assessed that the home next door was that of the Fuchs.

"How very convenient," he murmured, as he along with Holmes and Watson vacated the cab. "If I'm not mistaken, the two garages share a connecting wall, making it all too easy for either Friedl or Tobias free entry into the other person's home sight unseen."

Millicent pried herself from the front seat and looked up at the two homes seated on a small rise of land. At first glance, there appeared to be nothing unusual about the homes, but on further inspection, she could see that the Fuchs's residence was in much need of repair compared to that of their neighbor.

Before Alfredo could excuse the taxi, the driver sped off, leaving the four standing alone on the nearby sidewalk.

The Case of the Magic Fluke

"Well, it's now or never," she said determinedly, "let's go pay Herr Tichendorff a much needed visit."

Alfredo could see that it was becoming more and more difficult for his very pregnant wife to negotiate stairs, hills, and getting in and out of cars. "Are you sure you're up for this, *mia cara*?" he asked gently.

"Oh, I wouldn't miss it for the world," she answered, trying her best to hide a slight grimace of pain.

It wasn't until they got up to the Tichendorff door that she began to feel that same unusual queasiness in her stomach again. Then just as Alfredo was poised to knock, she abruptly stopped his arm with her hand and whispered, "I think the door is unlocked, Alfredo. I can feel it already in my body. And it tells me that what's behind the door is not going to be a pleasant sight."

Over the last few months Alfredo had learned to listen to his wife's premonitions and knew that often they turned out to be all too true. With his hand now gloved, he slowly turned the door knob to open the door a crack. "Hallo, Herr Tichendorff?" he called out. "It's me, Alfredo Martolini. Millicent and I have come merely to talk. No need to be afraid or apprehensive. We mean no harm, only to gather as much information as we can about the murder of Felix Fuchs."

No answer.

Alfredo took in a deep breath while Holmes and Watson stood readied

170

for whatever may be before them once inside the house. Millicent, now dizzy, put her hands up onto the doorjamb to steady herself.

"Okay, Herr Tichendorff," Alfredo continued, "I'm counting to three, and then coming in. Une . . . due . . . tre . . . ."

The door opened and there in front of them in the middle of the living room floor lay Tobias Tichendorff in a pool of his own blood—dead, as they say, as a door nail.

Alfredo rushed to check the man's pulse, while at the same time Millicent let out two *hiccups* and four *ah-choos* before passing out, falling backwards straight onto the lawn like a collapsible ironing board.

The dogs at once went berserk—Watson incessantly licking her face, while Holmes flew into the house, clamping down onto Alfredo's glove with his prominent underbite, and growling vociferously.

"Never mind him," he grumbled through clenched teeth, "Millicent is the one who needs your help now."

Without a moment's hesitation, Alfredo stormed back out the door and kneeled at the body of his now semi-comatose wife. "No, Millicent, no," he cried. "Don't leave us now. We need you. We love you. I love you, my darling. Please wake up."

In Holmes's mind it seemed that he was the only one of the three with any sort of brain function when it came to making decisions and carrying them through. Without forethought, he scurried into Millicent's tote in an effort to locate her mobile. Once found, he grabbed it by his teeth and ran with it toward Alfredo and dropped it at the man's knees.

"Call the police," he barked as he hopped up and down to get his master's attention. "And call for an ambulance. And while you're at it, call Mr. Smythe."

Chapter 12

Millicent looked around inside what she perceived was a backyard shed—her backyard shed. Well, not exactly *her* backyard shed, as she not only didn't have a backyard shed to her name, nor a backyard either, for that matter. No, this was the backyard shed of the person who was about to poison her husband, the criminal Friedl Fuchs.

Usually when she went into one of her episodes, she actually became the criminal in body and mind. Now, for some reason or another, Millicent was not only enacting the role of the criminal, but observing as herself, Millicent, as well. It was like she had two brains—that of Friedl and that of her—functioning at the same time.

As Friedl, she focused on constructing and delivering the rat poison cocktail which would soon obliterate her husband and at the same time her marriage, while simultaneously, as Millicent, she breathed a sigh of relief. Not only was her crime-solving talent in full force as she began to see the crime as it was taking place from her eyes as the criminal, but it had mutated into something quite extraordinary. She was able now to not only observe the crime, but anticipate and reflect at the same time as it was happening.

***

Woo-hoo, she muttered, causing Holmes, Watson, and Alfredo to stare down at her in disbelief.

"Did you hear what I just heard?" Alfredo asked incredulously.

"I believe our dear lady mumbled something sounding like a *woo-hoo*," Holmes answered gobsmacked.

"Yeah," Watson echoed, "*woo-hoo*."

"Stay by her side, boys, while I make my phone calls," Alfredo ordered. "And don't disturb her. She's obviously in one of her episodes, so we need to be diligent, making sure she stays safe and returns to us with whatever information she may glean from this experience."

Holmes could tell that Alfredo was more worried than he'd let on, so he did as he was told and stood watch over his mistress.

***

Millicent watched as she brought the freshly made concoction into the kitchen of her home. *I've got to pay attention now, so that I can remember how it is she was able to poison her unknowing husband.*

Ever so carefully she surveyed Friedl as the woman assembled one of Felix's and Millicent's favorite desserts—apple strudel. Quickly, Millicent pared the apples in front of her and sliced them into neat identical segments. Adding now the cocktail mixture to the apples, she also added a few rum-soaked raisins to hide whatever flavor the poison may be having on the fruit. No use getting caught before Felix had his fill.

Setting that aside, she next buttered the pre-made rectangle of phyllo dough before sprinkling breadcrumbs over the top. Carefully, Friedl drained the fruit of any residue liquid before laying it on the dough. Then, slowly and meticulously, she rolled the dough from the top toward her, careful not to tear the dough, which could easily allow the poisoned cocktail to seep out of the dessert and thus lose its potential lethality.

Soon Millicent heard herself sing something she faintly remembered from her past. If she was not mistaken, the tune sounded a great deal like Papageno's first aria from *The Magic Flute.*

"Here's your little song all about you, dear Felix," she sneered. "I hope you enjoy the ditty, for it will undoubtedly be the last thing you hear before your curtain goes down."

The bird-catcher, that's me,

always cheerful, hip hooray!

As a bird-catcher I'm known

to young and old throughout the land.

I'd like a net for girls,

I'd catch them for myself by the dozen!

Then I'd lock them up with me,

and all the girls would be mine.

Why Millicent remembered the German aria in English was momentarily beyond her. But by the time she'd finished singing, the poisoned phyllo was ready for the oven. That's when she felt herself stretch her arms and legs before turning over onto her side, mumbling as she did the phrase *apple strudel*.

***

Alfredo was about to call Mr. Smythe, when Millicent out of nowhere turned over to her side. All three males stared at her, anticipating that she may be waking up, but no dice. Millicent was still out cold.

"Oik think oi 'eard her burble somphin' sounding loike *apple strudel*. Anyone else 'ear that too?" Watson asked.

"Of course we did," Holmes said impatiently. "We're not deaf, merely deeply concerned about her and her baby's health."

"Why in the world is she asking for *apple strudel* at a time like this?" Alfredo asked. "I've heard of pregnancy cravings, but this is ridiculous."

Watson sidled over to where Holmes was sitting. "Do you suppose 'e's now able to understand us?" he whispered.

"I wish I understood her meaning," Alfredo continued. "I mean, does she want apple strudel, is she making apple strudel, or is *apple strudel* a code word for something we should have already figured out? I don't think I'll ever understand that woman."

"But you love her just the same, correct?" Holmes asked. Alfredo sighed deeply, lost in his thoughts. "But I love her just the same."

Holmes turned to his littermate. "Does that answer your question?" he asked smugly.

Watson merely sneezed and stretched out his back legs. "Yeah," he said, "I mean, no, not really."

***

As soon as Millicent turned over onto her side, she straight away remembered that in the dead of night with the help of her lover, Tobias Tichendorff, she'd carried the recently dead Felix Fuchs out of the Tichendorff work van and up two flights of stairs to the birth home apartment of Mozart. Her diabolical laughter rang out as she complimented herself on how without Gisela's knowledge she'd earlier in the week at a soccer practice stolen the keys to the museum from her purse.

Tee-hee-hee.

Tobias thought it would be funny if they'd set Felix's body into a sitting position at the Mozart family dining table, but she refused to dignify her husband in such a manner. Instead, she chose the Mozart piano as his final resting place.

Millicent played out the scene in her mind, watching Friedl closely as she and Tobias lifted the already stiff body of her husband onto the piano strings. At first they placed him into the piano face down, but that didn't sit well for Friedl. No, she wanted him to be found face up, with his feet sticking prominently out from under the piano lid, as if he were already lying in his coffin.

Then as the two swiftly left the Geburtshaus, Millicent heard herself victoriously singing the signature motif from the first movement of Mozart's Fortieth Symphony in G minor, but with lyrics of Friedl's own creation.

It's a bird, it's a plane, it's a Mozart, da-da dum, da-da dum, da-da dum.

"Wha' in the world?" Watson yipped nervously.

"Stay with her, Watson," Holmes ordered. "You know as well as I that when our dear Millicent's in the middle of an episode, it does not bode well for her or us if she should awaken."

"Right, yeah, awaken," he answered, curling his body up against her very pregnant tummy as comfort.

Alfredo, now on the phone to Mr. Smythe, related to him the goings on of Millicent's outbursts and the dogs' reactions to them.

"Is she all right?" Mr. Smythe asked, obviously concerned.

"I think so," Alfredo answered. "But I think we'll all rest better once

Friedl Fuchs is caught and brought to justice."

"Right," Mr. Smythe agreed, "I'll notify the Salzburg police to be on the lookout. And I'll make sure an officer with a forensics team is sent to the Tichendorff home to examine the body as well as the crime scene post haste."

"Thank you, Mr. Smythe."

"Please, call me *Bucky*."

Alfredo winced. He'd be hard put to answer to a boss named *Bucky*, but with Millicent as his wife, there seemed to always be a first time for everything.

"Yes, of course, Bucky," he said and placed his mobile back into his shirt pocket.

***

No sooner had Millicent sang her little ditty, than she turned over again, this time onto her opposite side. Not an easy feat for one as pregnant as she. As soon as she did, however, she felt the earlier sense of joy and victory now being replaced by intense feelings of fear and anger.

Grrrrr.

She looked down at her hand, now holding her husband Felix's pistol. "I'm sorry, Tobias, but I'm afraid you're going to have to go as well," she said as Friedl.

"But I thought we did all this so that we could at last be together," he said, pleading for his life. "I love you, Friedl."

"You actually thought I killed my husband so I could partner up with another idiot man such as yourself?" she asked, incredulously. "I need to be free, Tobias. Free to live my own life without the dictates of some man, or boss, or dumb male-oriented rules of FIFA."

Millicent noticed her hand holding the gun was beginning to shake. "So, here's where our story ends, Tobias. Sorry."

"But—"

Bang!

The gun went off and Millicent instantaneously sat up where she'd been lying.

Alfredo and Holmes quickly joined Watson at her side. "Millicent, my darling, are you all right?" Alfredo asked, taking her into his arms. "We've been so worried about you."

"Oh, for Pete's sake," she said, smiling. "I'm perfectly fine. And have I ever got a story to tell you."

***

Once finished with their energies at the crime scene, Millicent and Alfredo, along with Holmes and Watson, were given a ride back to their hotel by the Salzburg police. By then everyone was worn out and starved, so Alfredo broke down and ordered carry-out pizza for the four of them— two pizzas with *salame piccante* for him and the boys, and one vegetarian thin-crust pizza in a white garlic sauce for Millicent, heavy on the cheese.

"Oh, Alfredo," Millicent chattered away, her mouth full of pizza, "it was remarkable. Not only has my ability to have visions returned, but now I actually see the crime occurring through the eyes of the assailant, and at the same time as Millicent, observing the events from a witness's point of view."

"*Straordinario*," Alfredo replied, "extraordinary."

"And," Millicent went on, "I feel great. Much better than I've ever felt whenever in the past having gone through one of my so-called episodes"

Alfredo knew Millicent was telling the truth as far as she knew it. But he still couldn't help wondering if all the success they were having was ultimately too good to be true. No one save Holmes and Watson believed in Millicent's abilities more than he, but something still niggled in the back of his mind. And that niggling had much to do with not only Friedl Fuchs still being on the loose, but also the disappearance of Inspector Prachi Pesseingimpel.

Yet not wanting to bring sour grapes to the table, he kept his concerns to himself while amping up his vigilance regarding the safety and health of his wife and future child.

"So, maybe tomorrow we can go on that hike through the Alps you promised," Millicent said. "We did after all come here to enjoy the arts and culture as well as the great outdoors."

The Case of the Magic Fluke

Holmes abruptly stopped eating, while Watson whined, his front paws covering his face.

"Let's see how we all feel in the morning and make our decision from there," Alfredo suggested, noting the dogs' reactions to her plans. "It also might be nice for us instead to spend the day relaxing at the Bad Reichenhall resort. I've never been, and I'm sure the boys have not either."

Holmes went back to chowing down his pizza, while Watson uncovered his eyes and smiled. At least, Alfredo thought it was a smile—hard to tell those things on a push-face pug.

"All right," Millicent agreed, "we did after all come here to rest and recuperate from our busy year. It was merely a fluke that we ended up having to take on a case, and an extremely difficult one at that."

"Sì, but magical nonetheless," Alfredo said with a smile and then a giggle. "I guess you could call this caper 'the case of the magic fluke'."

Millicent groaned. "That's terrible. Mozart is probably at this moment rolling over in his grave."

Soon she and Holmes laughingly joined in Alfredo's mirth.

"Wassa *fluke*, 'olmes," Watson asked, perplexed.

Holmes rolled his eyes. "It means something that happens by chance, like our holiday in Salzburg leading to the Felix Fuchs case being solved. Without our presence, who knows how this investigation would have gone."

182

0

"Oh, yeah," Watson said, "you mean by lucky chance."

***

That night Millicent had no trouble falling asleep. Within seconds she could feel her shoulders relax and her breathing slow down to a steady pace. Before long she felt a strange side to side rocking of the bed, all too familiar to one who's had the opportunity in their life to ride a camel. Not once in her life had she ridden a camel, but if she had, this is probably what it would feel like, she presupposed.

Soon she noted a man with a black cigarette in his mouth and dressed in Bedouin attire, complete with a large headcloth, a long flowing kaftan, and a colorful cloak, riding forward on his camel, and pulling up on her right side.

"Monsieur H (pronounced *ahsh*), what are you doing here?" she asked. "For that matter, what exactly am *I* doing here?"

"Bonjour Madam Martolini," he greeted, "I am merely taking advantage of these lovely temperate summer nights in the desert to gather my thoughts as I enjoy the brilliance of the stars. See how close they are to the horizon?"

"Oh my," she said, looking up at the night sky, "they appear as if we could easily reach out and touch them."

"*Exactement, ma chérie*," he answered. "Yet do not be swept away by the desert's beauty, for underneath lurk many dangers, some of which are lethal indeed."

"Oh, all right," she answered, while looking nervously around her. "So what are you saying? Am I still in some kind of danger?"

"All I am saying, my dear, is that all the glitters is not gold, beware of wolves in sheep's clothing, and look both ways before crossing the street."

"Uh . . . okay, I think," she answered. "I'll do my best, Monsieur H, to keep that in mind."

"*Très bien*," he yelled back as his speedy camel took off ahead of her. "And don't go anywhere without Holmes and Watson. They're not only your good luck charms but are duty-bound to keep you safe."

"*Au revoir*, Monsieur H," she hollered, "I promise you I'd never leave those two behind."

A wave of nausea suddenly overtook her. Thinking it was merely the result of the camel ride, she talked herself into sitting up before making a quick exit to the kitchen for a glass of water. Yet as soon as she opened her eyes, she could see that her tummy issue had nothing to do with a camel, but rather Alfredo's jiggling of their bed.

"Millicent, my love," he said sleepily, "you must be dreaming. Turn over, my darling, close your beautiful eyes, and go back to sleep."

And she did just that.

Chapter 13

The next morning Millicent had woken up far too early. She'd slept hard after her dream-time visit from Monsieur H (pronounced *ahsh*), proven by the imprint of her wrinkled sheet against her cheek. Not wanting to disturb Alfredo, who was still fast asleep, but snoring lightly as was his habit soon before awakening, she slid out of bed and quietly tip-toed toward the loo.

"Oh bullocks," she said, looking at her face in the bathroom mirror. "I'd hoped since I'd finally solved the case yesterday that I would've slept better, or at least longer," she mumbled. Suddenly feeling as though she was being watched, she looked beyond the bathroom door and there the two of them sat, Holmes and Watson, waiting patiently until their mistress took notice of them.

Holmes was the first to speak. "Good morning, madam," he said,

The Case of the Magic Fluke

"I pray you slept well."

"Yeah," Watson added, "slept well."

Millicent looked down at the pair, a smile automatically forming on her face. "Well, I've slept better," she said, bending down once again to scratch behind their ears, "but I've also slept a whole lot worse. And how about you two, how did you sleep?"

"Not too bad," Holmes said, "except I had the most extraordinary dream. I don't remember much about it now, but I do recall that it had something to do with the Sahara Desert."

"Yeah," Watson agreed, "me too—the Sahara Desert and an obnoxious camel. Did you know they spit at small dogs for no particular reason other than they can?"

Millicent had a flash of something familiar, but she was hard pressed to remember what it was. "Well, the three of us are awake now, so we might as well get dressed and go outside for our morning constitutional. But let's be quiet about it. Alfredo plans to sleep in today, and I don't want to disturb him."

This sounded good to the boys, so they trotted over to the front door where they waited patiently for Millicent to dress and gather her things—like her phone in case Alfredo called, a key to the suite so they could get back in, and a few Euros should they happen upon a bakery or pretzel wagon on their journey.

When finally dressed and ready, she hooked both Holmes and Watson up to their leads, trotted out into the hallway, and quietly closed the door behind her. "Now," she said sweetly, "we can make all the noise we want. The sun, like us, is already up, promising another beautiful summer's day here in Salzburg."

As the three climbed into the lift, Holmes and Watson noted that Millicent was whistling what sounded vaguely familiar from their first evening's encounter at the Marionette Theater.

"'ey 'olmes, doesn't that sound like Mozart to you?" he asked

Holmes recognized it immediately as the bird catcher's aria from the first act. "Of course, it sounds like Mozart, because it is Mozart. One of the puppets in the opera we attended our first evening here sang it. That was, until you attacked the stage and completely destroyed it, forcing us to leave the premises before the production had ended."

"Yeah," Watson snickered, "before it ended."

The lift stopped on the lobby floor, allowing Millicent and the dogs to trot passed the concierge desk before zipping out the door. There at his post stood Reinhardt Rauscher.

"Guten Morgen, Frau Martolini," he said politely, "it looks like you three are up early and ready to greet the day."

"Why, yes we are," she said smilingly, "thank you so much for noticing." And out the glass front doors they went.

The Case of the Magic Fluke

The chill of the morning mountain air did its job of helping Millicent wake up and take note of the many different kinds of birds chirping in the trees. Jays, jackdaws, and ravens joined in chorus with a host of sparrows, pipits, and chaffinches, making the morning feel alive with song.

"How can Alfredo possibly want to sleep in on such a lovely day as this, huh boys?" she asked as she released their leads. Holmes was a sniffer, and enjoyed nothing better than to put his nose to the ground so as to explore the different kinds of odors and scents discovered while roaming the park lands. Watson, on the other hand, tended to look upward and chase whatever it was that caught his fancy, be it butterfly, bee, or feather—basically anything carried by the wind.

After several minutes Millicent returned the dogs to their leashes and was about to head back to the hotel when her mobile rang. Not recognizing the number, she decided nonetheless to answer it.

"Hallo?" she asked curiously.

"Frau Martolini, this is Inspector Pesseingimpel. Can we talk?"

Millicent stopped frozen in her tracks. "Prachi, is it really you? I've been calling you nonstop since you picked up up at the hospital, and you've yet to return any of my calls."

"Yes," she said, "I'm so sorry about that. I've been tied up since then."

"Well, you had us so worried, that we finally had to report you missing to the Salzburg Missing Persons Bureau. Is everything all right? I notice the number you're calling from is not that of your mobile."

"What I'm calling you about has to do with the Fuchs case," she said. Millicent thought the inspector sounded somewhat strained but was too interested in what she had to say than to think much further about it.

"Yes, and what about the Fuchs case?"

"I've recently discovered some pertinent information, but I don't feel comfortable mentioning it over the phone. Do you think you could meet me somewhere this morning for a quick chat?"

Millicent thought about it for a minute. She knew she really should get back to the hotel and have Alfredo come with her to speak with the woman, but there was no time like the present. Besides, she was already up and dressed, whereas Alfredo was most likely still in bed. And it wasn't as if she were meeting her by herself. Why, Holmes and Watson were with her, and she knew they'd do their best to protect her or die trying.

"I guess that would be all right," she finally said. "Any place in particular?"

"Yes, what I have to show you is at the Hohensalzburg Castle, the fortress that you see at the top of the hill above the old town square."

The instant Millicent heard the words *Hohensalzburg Castle* she grew excited. She'd been meaning to make that one of her and Alfredo's sightseeing destinations, but they hadn't had much time to fit it into their itinerary given the case they'd been assigned.

"Yes, that sounds perfect," she said.

"Good," the inspector sighed, "take the Festungsbahn Funicular at the base of the hill, and I'll meet you at the top."

"Brilliant," Millicent answered, "see you soon." At once Millicent used her speed dial to call for a taxi. Any other time she would've walked the distance, but she was now in a hurry. And there was no point wearing her and the boys out before arriving at the castle. Besides, it was enough that they were making this trip without having breakfast, which she assured herself she'd purchase as soon as she could.

***

The taxi made swift progress through the early morning streets of Salzburg. In fact, it was no surprise to Millicent that the line for the funicular was all but missing, save for an old woman waiting nearby.

"Come on, boys," she said to Holmes and Watson, "the sooner we get to the castle and meet the inspector, the sooner we can go get something to eat."

The three of them scampered onto the train and rushed to each find window seats in which to sit. Just as the doors were about to close, the old woman jumped on as well. Millicent thought nothing of it. Yet as soon as the woman scooted past Holmes to find her seat, he began to growl.

"What is it, boy?" Millicent asked. "You aren't afraid of a silly funicular, are you?"

Then, always a dollar short and a day late, Watson started to growl as well.

Suddenly the train lurched forward to begin its ascent.

"What's up with you two?" Millicent continued. "I've never known you to be quite so squeamish."

"It's probably because I have my gun pointed at your head," said the voice of the woman seated behind her.

What is the world? Wait. I know that voice.

"Why Friedl Fuchs," Millicent said at last, "I wondered when we would run into each other again."

"You didn't think I'd let you get away with turning me into the police, did you?" she asked bitterly.

"Well, after all you did murder your husband," Millicent reasoned. "And if I'm not mistaken, your neighbor Tobias Tichendorff as well. Correct me if I'm wrong."

"No, you're not wrong. Those two idiots didn't even know what hit them," she said sarcastically with a chortle. She then nuzzled the barrel of the gun against the back of Millicent's neck. "And if it wasn't for you and that gorgeous husband of yours, I'd have gotten away with it."

"Uhm, I don't think so," Millicent argued.

The Case of the Magic Fluke

"Shut up," Friedl snarled, "Gisela was my perfect patsy, but you had to spoil everything with your constant questioning and whatever else you use in your detective work."

Millicent saw that Holmes and Watson in order to protect her were about to pounce. Not wanting them to get hurt, however, she quickly brought them close to her lap and held them there.

"I simply follow the clues, and you most certainly left behind a slew of them."

"Ha, did not!"

"Did so," Millicent answered, doing her best to throw the woman off course, "so *ha* yourself."

"That's it," Friedl shouted, "I've had more than enough of you and your *spielereien*." And with that she wrapped Millicent on the back of the head with the butt of her pistol, knocking her silly, yet shutting her up nonetheless.

***

The first thing Alfredo did after waking was glance at his watch. It was already mid-morning. "Millicent?" he called out, "Holmes? Watson? Anybody here?"

No answer.

Ah, they must have gone outside or down to the hotel restaurant for breakfast, he thought. Feeling rested, he quickly took his shower, shaved, and dressed for the relaxing afternoon he planned on having. And since his wife and the pugs had still not returned, he decided to go down and meet them at the restaurant. He took his mobile, his wallet, and his morning sweater just in case they all decided to go somewhere fun.

When he arrived at the restaurant, however, he noticed that it was closed for breakfast and wouldn't open again until noon for lunch or supper.

That's odd, he thought, *I wonder what's taking them so long to return from where it is they went.*

He decided to take a look outside. Perhaps they were playing on the lawn—sniffing around or chasing butterflies. First he made a stop at the concierge desk.

"Buongiorno, Reinhardt," he said to the young man at his post. "You haven't happened to have seen my wife this morning, have you signore?"

Reinhardt looked up from his desk. "Why, yes," he said, "I saw her and your two pets leave the building a few hours ago. Has she not returned as yet?"

Alfredo felt the heat of fear crawl up his neck. "No, she hasn't. Nor have the dogs. Excuse me, while I make a phone call."

Within seconds Alfredo pulled out his mobile and called Millicent's cell. It went immediately to voice mail. "Millicent, my love, please call me as soon as you get this message," he said.

He waited for her call, but after five minutes he realized that she may be in real trouble. Again he placed a call, this time to Mr. Smythe, who picked up his private mobile at the first ring.

"Good morning, Alfredo," he said, "what can I do for you?"

"It's Millicent—she along with Holmes and Watson are missing, and I have no idea where they have gone."

"Meet me at the Salzburg Police Station helipad. I should be there within ten minutes.

And don't worry, Alfredo, I and the FIFA Security Council are on it," Mr. Smythe said and hung up.

***

When Millicent finally came to, she discovered both her hands and feet had been bound in plastic ties, and that she was roped back to back with Inspector Prachi Pesseingimpel, whose hands and feet likewise had been bound. They were both in one of the castle's stone-walled rooms.

"I'm sorry I called you up here, Millicent," Prachi said, "but I had no choice. Friedl threatened to shoot me otherwise."

"So you've been up here the entire time?" Millicent asked.

"I'm afraid so. After you left the hospital, I went and spoke to Gisela Gruber and then from there checked in with Friedl to make sure she was doing all right. Unfortunately, she was a few steps ahead of me. Honestly, I didn't for a minute suspect her of anything, and so I ended up as easy prey."

"I see," Millicent said, noticing that Holmes and Watson had curled themselves protectively onto her lap.

"She only untied me long enough for me to make that phone call to you, and later to help her carry you off the funicular and into this room."

Millicent looked around as best she could for the room was lit by only one small candle. "This room looks like a chapel of some kind," she said.

"That's exactly what it is," Prachi said. "St. George's Chapel located here at the Hohensalzburg Fortress."

"Why, it's beautiful, but I'd still rather not be here."

"I can imagine. Here you and Alfredo are trying to enjoy a holiday, and by some fluke you end up having to work on yet another difficult and time-consuming case, not to mention possibly dying," Prachi said sympathetically.

"It can't be easy for you either, Prachi, new to the force and having your life cut short before you even get started. Somehow this whole thing seems incredibly unfair."

Prachi began to tear up. "At least I can say I worked on a case with the infamous Millicent Winthrop, even though the villain is still at large."

"Well, I for one am happy to have gotten to know you," Millicent said with a sniffle, "even though our relationship looks as though it will be severely cut short."

The Case of the Magic Fluke

***

As if out of the blue, Watson abruptly stood up from her lap and began to yip and dance around. "What's that sound I 'ear, 'olmes? It sounds remarkably like a typhoon. Although I've never 'eard a typhoon before, I can only guess that this is wha' it may sound like."

"I say, dear lady," Holmes said, jumping up and down with glee, "I believe those are police helicopters I hear. Perhaps we're being rescued after all."

"Oh, I do hope so," Millicent squealed, "being shot would be horrible, but starving to death would be even worse. And I could really go for a slice of apple strudel right now."

At that moment Salzburg's finest came running into the chapel with Mr. Smythe and Alfredo close behind. Mr. Smythe swiftly undid the inspector's bindings, while Alfredo did the same for Millicent.

"I'm so sorry, Alfredo," she said, smiling and crying at the same time. "I had no idea this was going to happen, but at least you were free and able to notify Bucky and the police that Holmes and Watson and I had gone missing."

"Ah, Millicent, *mia cara*, I am not angry," Alfredo said, covering her in kisses. "I'm just so happy you and the boys and the baby are safe and back in my arms." He then helped his lovely wife up onto her feet, but as soon as he did, Millicent bent over in pain, crying out as if she'd been

196

attacked by a swarm of killer wasps.

"Oooooohhhhhhh," she moaned.

"What is it, darling? Your back? Your legs? Your feet?"

"Nooooohhhhhh," she groaned again. "It's our baby. Oh, Alfredo, I think it's time."

***

Alfredo stood frozen, at a loss as to what to do next.

"Stand back, Alfredo," Mr. Smythe at once ordered. "Let the police assist Millicent into the helicopter without further delay so we can transport the two of you along with Holmes and Watson to the nearby local hospital."

Mamma mia, mamma mia, mamma mia was all Alfredo could repeatedly say as the four of them were at once lifted off the hill and rushed to their next destination.

"Was going on, 'olmes?" Watson asked as they were in mid-flight.

Holmes rolled his eyes for the umpteenth time—then smiled up at his ever-curious brother. "We're going to soon receive a baby niece or nephew. What do you think about that?"

Watson thought about it for a second. "I 'ope the baby takes more after me than it will you," he said with a mischievous look in his eye.

"Why you . . . ." Holmes said, allowing his dear brother Watson to chase him up one side of the helicopter and down the other.

Epilogue

It wasn't what they'd planned, nor was it what the two had hoped for, but the minute Millicent went into serious labor, Alfredo passed out cold. Rushed to a room of his own where he could be looked after, Alfredo had missed nearly all the details of his baby's birth. At first Millicent was disappointed, but after giving it some thought, she realized it was actually quite amusing—that tall, gorgeous, brave, and heroic husband of hers was finally brought down by a slightly less than three kilogram bundle of joy.

Holmes and Watson, of course, were by her side during the entire event. And Mr. Smythe must have checked up on her at least a dozen times before, during, and after the baby's arrival. Even the entire hospital staff was more than helpful by taking the baby to the nursery soon after it had arrived, allowing Millicent to grab a quick nap.

At last, Alfredo awoke and was immediately rushed by wheelchair to Millicent side.

"My darling, can you ever forgive me?" he blubbered as he crawled up into her bed to hold her. "I feel like such a fool."

"Don't be silly, Alfredo," she said smiling, "you have made me the happiest woman on this earth. But you'd better hurry up and kiss me, for our little surprise is about to make its entrance." Alfredo swiftly took Millicent into his arms to deepen his kiss when they were at once interrupted.

"Congratulations, Herr Martolini. You are now the proud father of a beautiful baby girl," the head nurse said, handing the little bundle of love over to him.

Alfredo took one look at his baby daughter, and his heart melted. The fuzz on her head was as brown as his, but her eyes were every bit Millicent's blue. And when she opened them to look at her papa, he wept for joy.

"And you have made me the happiest man in the universe, my wonderful, clever, and oh so loved, Millicent."

AUSTRIAN RECIPES OF SALZBURG

Cunigunda *Valentine*

Apple Strudel

Though a popular dessert in many European countries, apple strudel dates from 1697 and has its origin in Austria.

Ingredients

<u>The Dough</u>

2 ½ c. all-purpose flour

¼ tsp. salt

2 T. plus 1 tsp. vegetable oil

13 T. lukewarm water

<u>The First Filling</u>

7 T. butter

1 c. breadcrumbs

<u>The Second Filling</u>

½ c. raisins

4 T/ rum or orange juice

6-8 c. chopped baking apples

3-4 c. granulated sugar

1-2 tsp. lemon zest

4 T. lemon juice

¼ tsp. cinnamon

1 whole stick of melted butter for brushing the dough

Powdered sugar for decoration

The Case of the Magic Fluke

Preparation

To make the dough: Place the flour in a bowl with the salt and add the water, then the oil. Stir with a spoon until it comes together and you can work it with your hands. Knead the dough until it is smooth and tacky, but not sticky, about 5 minutes. If you need to add more flour, only add it 1 teaspoon at a time. Form the dough into a smooth ball, brush it with a little oil and place it back in the bowl for 1 hour, room temperature.

Make Filling I: Heat the butter in a pan until foaming and add the breadcrumbs. Toast them, stirring constantly, until they are medium brown. Let cool.

Make Filling II: Soak the raisins in the rum (or orange juice). You can heat them for 30 seconds in the microwave and then soak them until you are ready for them. Peel, core and chop the apples into small pieces. Add the sugar, lemon juice, lemon zest, raisins and cinnamon and mix well.

Roll out the dough on a lightly floured board to about 9 inches by 13 inches. Lightly flour a clean towel with no nap, place it over the dough, grab both (towel and dough) and flip over. Straighten both, as necessary. Using your hands, gently stretch the dough thinner on all sides, working your way around the sheet of dough. Stretch it until it starts to look translucent in spots. Let it rest a minute and stretch the areas you think are too thick, again. Thick edges can't be avoided and will be cut off. Brush dough with melted butter.

Spread the breadcrumbs over 2/3 of the dough and pat down evenly. Drain the apples and spread them over the other 1/3 of the dough. Cut off any thick edges of dough with kitchen shears. Using the towel, fold one side of the dough over the filling. Brush exposed dough with melted butter. Fold in ends of dough like an envelope (or burrito). Fold other side of dough up and over filling to form a roll. Brush with butter. Use towel to maneuver strudel to baking sheet lined with parchment paper. Roll strudel onto parchment paper so that the seam-side is down. Brush with melted butter.

Bake at 400°F for 20 minutes and then at 350°F for 40-60 minutes longer. Remove from oven, brush top with melted butter and sprinkle with powdered sugar while still warm. Transfer to a serving platter with a large spatula (or two). Cut into 1 1/2 inch wide slices with a bread knife or serrated knife and serve with your choice of whipped cream, vanilla sauce, or vanilla ice cream.

Tips: If you are planning on serving the strudel the next day, leave on parchment paper and cover loosely with a clean kitchen towel. Place out of reach. Re-crisp in oven, warming in microwave not as good.

Practice making strudel before you want to serve it. Make it at least once before the big day to see which steps you need to watch.

Err on the side of thicker dough. If you stretch it too thin before you put the filling in, when you wrap it you will stretch it more, and it might tear. Tearing causes the liquid to evaporate when baked, instead of steaming inside the package. It won't ruin your strudel, but it will not be perfect.

Erdäpfelgulasch

Ingredients

4 big or 7 medium starchy potatoes (russets or yellow)

3 medium yellow onions

1 clove garlic

2 large smoked sausages

2 tablespoons and 1 tsp. Hungarian paprika

2 teaspoons vinegar 1 tablespoon tomato paste

1 teaspoon marjoram

1 3/4 teaspoon caraway seeds, ground medium-fine

3/4 teaspoon coriander seeds, ground medium-fine

1/2 teaspoon sugar

1/2 teaspoon fine salt

1/2 teaspoon freshly ground pepper

2 bay leaves

1 bouillon cube (for 2 cups broth)

7-8 cups water

Instructions

Peel, wash and cut the potatoes into 3/4 inch cubes.

Cut the onions in half lengthwise, and then finely slice them (half-rings).

Heat 2 tablespoons oil in a large pot, preferably non-stick. Add the onions and cook over high heat for 5 minutes. Stir constantly. After 5 minutes reduce heat to medium and cook onions, stirring often, for about 15 minutes, or until soft and golden to light-brown in color. Don't brown them too much as they will taste bitter.

Add garlic for the last 2 minutes (directly grate/press it into the pot).

Prepare a pot with 8 cups of hot water, you will gradually add later.

When the onions are golden, add both types of paprika. There should be enough oil in the pot, so the paprika won't burn (=bitter taste). Stir for 10 seconds and deglaze with vinegar.

Immediately add tomato paste, marjoram, caraway and coriander. Stir for a few seconds, then gradually add 1 cup of water while stirring. Allow the liquid to reduce, then add another cup of hot water. Boil it down to a creamy consistency. I like to get a smooth sauce, this is why I blend the sauce (I use a hand-held blender). You can skip the next step, if you want some onion chunks in the sauce.

Remove pot from the heat and let it cool down slightly. Puree in a blender or food processor, or very carefully (!) with a hand-held blender.

Put the onion-sauce back into the pot.

Add sugar, salt, pepper, bay leaves 1 crumbled bouillon cube.

With a ladle add all but about 1 cup of the hot water to the goulash (depending on your pot and heat, you will need the last cup). Stir each time after adding water.

Add the potato cubes and cook for 1/2 hour, without lid.

Meanwhile slice sausages (about 1/4 inch thick) and add. Cook another 30 minutes, until the potatoes are just done.

Fish out 15 to 20 potatoes, put them into a small bowl and thoroughly mash them with a fork. Add a ladle of the goulash sauce to the mashed potatoes, stir and, if needed, mash again so you will get a smooth paste.

Pour the mashed potato sauce back into the pot and cook for a couple more minutes. The sauce should thicken with this trick. If you let it cool and heat the goulash again, its consistency will be thicker.

Käsespätzle

A traditional dish from the German and Austrian regions of Swabia, Baden, Allgäu, Voralberg, and Tyrol. It's a favorite in Salzburg!

Ingredients

5 cups cooked Spätzle, can use store-bought if preferred

6 tablespoons butter

2 very large onions chopped

1/2 teaspoon salt

1/2 teaspoon sugar

12 ounces shredded Emmentaler or Jarlsberg cheese

Salt

Preparation

Preheat the oven to 400 degrees F. Butter a 9x13 (or a little smaller) casserole dish.

To make the caramelized onions: Melt the butter in a medium-sized heavy stock pot or Dutch oven. Add the onions and stir occasionally for 20-30 minutes until deeply caramelized. Halfway into it sprinkle with a little salt and sugar to help with the caramelizing. Get the onions nice and brown.

Layer 1/3 of the Spätzle in the bottom of the dish followed by 1/3 of the cheese and 1/3 of the caramelized onions. Repeat, sprinkling each layer with some salt, ending with cheese and onions on top.

Bake for 10 minutes or longer until the cheese is melted and the edges are just beginning to get a little crispy. Serve immediately.

Paprika Chicken

A very popular Salzburg dish of Hungarian origin and made with Hungarian Paprika. Can be served with a buckwheat side dish, although dumplings are the more common.

Ingredients

<u>Chicken and Dumplings</u>

$1\frac{1}{2}$ lbs boneless skinless chicken breasts

1 to 2 T oil

4 T paprika (Hungarian sweet is preferable)

3 T onion powder

2 tps salt

$\frac{1}{4}$ tps pepper

32 ounces chicken broth

10 ounces sour cream

$2\frac{1}{4}$ cups water

$\frac{3}{4}$ cup flour

<u>Dumplings</u>

6 eggs

4 cups flour

$1\frac{1}{2}$ cups water

$\frac{1}{2}$ teaspoon salt

Preparation

Set a large pot of water on to boil for the dumplings.

De-fat, and tenderize chicken. Cut into bite-sized pieces. With oil, brown chicken in a large pan on medium-high heat (6-10 min).

Add paprika, onion powder, salt, pepper, and chicken broth to the chicken in the pan. Stir them to mix. Bring to a boil and then lower heat to simmer and put a lid on and let simmer for 25 minute.

In a container with a lid mix water, flour and sour cream for the chicken. Shaking the mixture aggressively is the best way to ensure a smooth mix. Set aside mixture for later.

While chicken is simmering, mix all ingredients - eggs, flour, water, and salt - for the dumplings together in a mixing bowl. It should be a thick, dry mix when you are done. If it's too gooey, add small amounts of flour until it is more dry.

With water boiling, turn down the heat to low. Tip the mixing bowl until the dumpling dough rests at the edge. Using a dull knife (butter knife), slice the dough from the lip of the bowl into small blobs and into the pot. Continue this process until all of the dough has been used. This process takes about 3-5 minute Dipping the knife occasionally into the boiling water will prevent dough from sticking to it.

Raise heat and boil dumplings for another 5-6 min or so.

Meanwhile, the chicken should be about done simmering. Using a spoon, draw some of the chicken sauce and put it into the sour cream/flour/water mixture that you had set aside. This is important to prevent sour cream from curdling. Put the lid on and shake the mixture once more. There should be no flour or sour cream chunks in the mixture.

Finally, stir the mixture into the chicken pan. Mix until consistent.

Bring the sauce to a boil stirring occasionally for sauce to thicken.

Drain the water from the dumplings.

Usually, chicken and sauce are served on top of the dumplings.

Sachertorte

From the Hotel Sacher in Vienna comes this delicious dessert. It gets its name from its inventor, Franz Sacher, who supposedly prepared it in 1832 for Prince Metternich in Vienna. One of the most famous Austrian culinary specialties.

Ingredients

The Cake

6 large eggs, separated

1 c all-purpose flour

½ c almond flour

¼ tsp salt

1 ½ sticks unsalted butter, softened

1 c sugar

5 ounces bittersweet chocolate, melted and cooled slightly

Filling and Glaze

1 ¾ c apricot preserves

2/3 c light corn syrup

2 T rum

10 ounces bittersweet chocolate, chopped

Unsweetened whipped cream for serving

Preparation

Preheat the oven to 375°. Butter a 9-inch springform pan. Line the bottom of the pan with parchment paper and butter the paper. Dust the pan with flour, tapping out the excess.

In a large bowl, using a handheld electric mixer, whip the egg whites at high speed until soft peaks form. In a small bowl, whisk the all-purpose flour with the almond flour and salt. In another large bowl, beat the butter and sugar until fluffy. Add the yolks, one at a time, and beat until fluffy. Beat in the chocolate, then beat in the flours. Beat in one-fourth of the whites, then, using a spatula, fold in the rest of the whites until no streaks remain.

Scrape the batter into the prepared pan and smooth the top. Bake the cake in the center of the oven for 35 to 40 minutes, until a toothpick inserted in the center comes out with a few moist crumbs attached. Let the cake cool on a wire rack for 30 minutes, then remove the ring and let the cake cool completely. Invert the cake onto a plate and peel off the parchment. Turn the cake right side up. Using a long serrated knife, cut the cake horizontally into 3 even layers.

In a small microwave-safe bowl, whisk 1/4 cup plus 2 tablespoons of the apricot preserves with 1/4 cup of water and microwave until melted.

The Case of the Magic Fluke

Set the bottom of the springform pan on a wire rack and set the rack on a baking sheet. Arrange the top cake layer, cut side up, on the springform pan. Brush the cake with one-third of the melted apricot preserves. Spread 1/2 cup of the unmelted apricot preserves on top and cover with the middle cake layer. Brush the surface with another third of the melted preserves and spread another 1/2 cup of the unmelted preserves on top. Brush the cut side of the final layer with the remaining melted preserves and set it cut side down on the cake. Using a serrated knife, trim the cake edges if necessary to even them out.

In the microwave-safe bowl, microwave the remaining 1/4 cup plus 2 tablespoons of the apricot preserves until melted, about 30 seconds. Press the preserves through a strainer to remove the solids. Brush the preserves all over the cake until completely coated. Refrigerate for 20 minutes until set.

Meanwhile, in a medium saucepan, whisk the corn syrup with the rum and 2 tablespoons of water and bring to a boil. Cook until slightly thickened, about 1 minute. Put the chocolate into a heatproof bowl and pour the hot mixture on top. Let stand until melted, then whisk until smooth. If the chocolate glaze is too thick to pour, whisk in another tablespoon of hot water. Let cool to warm.

Using an offset spatula, scrape off any excess preserves from the cake so that it is lightly coated. Slowly pour half of the warm chocolate glaze in the center of the cake, allowing it to gently coat the top and spread down the side. Spread the glaze to evenly coat the torte. Microwave the remaining glaze for a few seconds and repeat pouring and spreading. Scrape up any excess glaze. Refrigerate for at least 10 minutes to set the glaze, then cut the torte into wedges and serve with the whipped cream.

The torte can be covered and refrigerated for up to 2 days.

Salzburger Nockerl

For some Austrians, Salzburger Nockerl may be nothing more than hot air whilst others may think it is the best dessert in the world. Hailing from the city of Mozart, this light and fluffy dessert may remind some people of Salzburg's snow capped-mountains.

Ingredients

½ cup of milk

½ vanilla pod

freshly squeezed lemon juice

7 egg whites

pinch of salt

¼ cup sugar

4 egg yolks

lemon zest

2 tsp vanilla sugar

2 tbsp flour

1 tbsp cornstarch

icing sugar for dusting

butter for greasing

Preparation

Begin by heating milk with cut-open vanilla pod and lemon juice over low heat.

Remove and discard vanilla pod. Butter an oval shaped, oven proof dish and pour in enough vanilla milk to cover bottom.

Hand mix cooled egg whites with pinch of salt and a third of sugar until very stiff.

Add remaining sugar slowly and beat until thick and creamy.

Preheat over 400°F. Add egg yolks, lemon zest, vanilla sugar, flour, and cornstarch to egg whites and fold a few times with whisk.

Make 3 pyramid-shaped nockerl and place them next to each other in baking dish.

Bake 10-12 minutes until golden brown. Dust with icing sugar and serve immediately.

Stuffed Lake Trout with Spinach

Ingredients

2 ⅕ pounds spinach

4 shallots

1 garlic

1 piece fresh ginger

7 ounces button mushroom

3 tomatoes

2 tablespoons olive oil

nutmeg

salt

peppers

1 bunch parsley

1 lemon

2 small steelhead trout (ready to cook, about 21-22 oz)

Preparation

Rinse spinach thoroughly, then trim stems and drain.

Peel shallots, garlic and ginger. Cut shallots into 8 pieces each and set aside 2 shallot pieces. Finely dice remaining shallots and the garlic and ginger.

Clean mushrooms, cut about half of them into slices and finely dice the rest.

Rinse and dry tomatoes and cut out stem. Cut tomatoes into quarters and dice finely.

Heat oil in a pot. Add shallot eighths, sliced mushrooms, garlic and ginger.

Add spinach and sauté, stirring, until wiltedr. Season with freshly grated nutmeg, salt and pepper. Fold in diced tomatoes and remove the pan from the heat.

Rinse the parsley, shake dry, pluck off the leaves and chop finely. Rinse lemon in hot water and wipe dry. Finely grate the zest. Cut lemon in half and squeeze juice.

Mix lemon zest and juice, diced mushrooms and shallots and the parsley in a small bowl.

Rinse trout and pat dry with paper towels inside and out. Season with salt and pepper. Fill with mushroom mixture and seal fish with toothpicks.

Lift spinach from the pan and spread in a baking dish. Lay trout on top and place any remaining filling around fish. Bake, covered with parchment paper, in a preheated oven at 400°F for about 35 minutes, then uncover and bake for approximately 18 minutes more. Serve immediately.

Tafelspitz

Boiled veal, or Tafelspitz, is the king of the beef dishes in Vienna. There is practically no more delicious proof of how firmly the Austrian cuisine is rooted in the heart of Europe than one of the most typical of Viennese dishes: boiled veal, or Tafelspitz. **Good-quality beef**, a few vegetables, **aromatic spices**, and plenty of water to cook in are the vital ingredients. The same ingredients as when the French are creating their "pot-au-feu" or the Italians their "bollito misto".

Cunigunda *Valentine*

Ingredients

Approx. 1.5 kg / 3.5 lb beef topside (or other quality boiling beef, such as centre cut rump, chuck beef or brisket)

beef bones, if desired

½ leek

1 large onion with skin

1-2 bay leaves

a few peppercorns

salt

Preparation

Slice the unpeeled onion in half widthways and fry off the cut surfaces without fat until fairly well browned.

Put around 3 litres of water into a large saucepan. Add the root vegetables, leek, halves of onion, bay leaves, and peppercorns and bring to a boil. Add the washed meat and bones and, depending on the type of meat, allow to **cook until softened** in gently simmering water, which will take around 2 1/2 – 3 hours. Add more water as required and skim off any foam from the surface.

Season well with salt, but only after a good 2 hours.

Once the meat has softened, remove it from the pan and keep it warm in some of the liquid from the soup. Season the remainder of the soup again with salt to taste, and strain it (optional). Serve with semolina dumplings or frittata and freshly chopped chives as a starter.

Slice the boiled beef by cutting on the bias and arrange on pre-heated plates, or serve in the hot soup in a decorative soup tureen.

Serve with roast potatoes, a bread and horseradish mix, green beans in a dill sauce, or creamed spinach and chive sauce. If the root vegetables are to be served at the same time, cook some of them separately to be served al dente.

Cooking time: approx. 2 1/2 – 3 hours

Wiener Schnitzel

The true origin of the Wiener Schnitzel has become a matter of vigorous debate between culinary historians. One thing, however, is absolutely certain: the Wiener Schnitzel is truly cosmopolitan. The earliest trails lead to Spain, where the Moors were coating meat with breadcrumbs during the Middle Ages. The Jewish community in Constantinople is similarly reported to have known a dish similar to the Wiener Schnitzel in the 12th century. So whether the legend surrounding the import of the "Costoletta Milanese" from Italy to Austria by Field Marshal Radetzky is true or merely a nice story makes very little difference, in actual fact. So long as the schnitzel is tender and crispy!

Ingredients

Veal cutlets

Salt & Pepper

Flour

Breadcrumbs

Eggs

Preparation

Lay out the cutlets, remove any skin and beat until thin. Season on both sides with salt and pepper. Place flour and breadcrumbs into separate flat plates, beat the eggs together on a further plate using a fork.

Coat each schnitzel on both sides in flour, then draw through the beaten eggs, ensuring that no part of the schnitzel remains dry. Lastly, coat in the breadcrumbs and carefully press down the crumbs using the reverse side of the fork (this causes the crumb coating to "fluff up" better during cooking).

In a large pan (or 2 medium-sized pans), **melt sufficient clarified butter** for the schnitzel to be able to swim freely in the oil (or heat up the plant oil with 1 – 2 tbsp of clarified butter or butter).

Only place the Schnitzel in the pan when the fat is so hot that it hisses and bubbles up if some breadcrumbs or a small piece of butter is introduced to it. Depending on the thickness and the type of meat, fry for between 2 minutes and 4 minutes until golden brown. Turn using a spatula (do not pierce the coating!) and fry on the other side until similarly golden brown.

The Case of the Magic Fluke

Remove the crispy schnitzel and place on kitchen paper to dry off. Dab carefully to dry the schnitzel. Arrange on the plate and garnish with slices of lemon before serving.

Serve with **parsley potatoes**, rice, potato salad or mixed salad.

Cooking time: depending on the thickness and the meat, 4 – 8 minutes

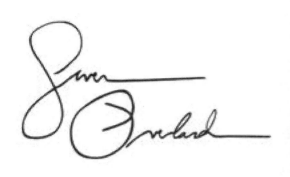

About Gwen Overland

After years in academia, writing one research article followed by another, Gwen turned her talents toward writing fiction and found she happily could not stop.

In addition to writing cozy mysteries as her pseudonym **Cunigunda Valentine**, Gwen also writes romance novels and has two published non-fiction books on the work she does in conjunction with her business, **Expressive Voice Dynamics: Soul of Voice** and **Soul of My Voice**.

She currently lives in Ashland, Oregon, home of the Oregon Shakespeare Festival, with her family and her beloved black pug. Prior to that, Gwen lived in Los Angeles and had careers in directing, acting, and singing while performing at the piano. She's a Puget Sound gal at heart though and you'll catch glimpses of this beautiful Washington area sprinkled throughout some of her books.

The **Millicent Winthrope** Series

Keep up with Gwen by following her on Twitter @gwenoverland; Gwen Overland Author on Facebook; @GwenOverland on Instagram, or at www.gwenoverland.com and www.cunigundavalentine.com.

Made in the USA
Middletown, DE
14 July 2024

57293956R00126